Best of Boehy

Thank so much

Joey M. Weil 4/10/10

i

Tye Watkins in

Back To The Rockies

Book Six of the Tye Watkins Series

By
Gary McMillan

Cover Concept and Design by Michael McMillan

Authors' Discovery Cooperation, Inc.
165 Cherry Lane
Robert Lee, Texas 76945
325-453-4595
Web: www.authorsdiscovery.com
e-mail: ldudney@nwol.net

Published by: Authors' Discovery Cooperation, Inc. February 2010

ISBN Number   978-0-9844730-0-7

Printed in the United States of America

OTHER BOOKS
IN THE
TYE WATKINS SERIES

The Mountain Man

The era of the mountain man was from the late 18th century to about mid-19th century when the demand for beaver fur had all but ceased. To be a mountain man was a little more complicated than just buying traps and heading to the Rockies. A lot of men died thinking they were going to get rich trapping beaver. The truth was that very few trappers got rich. As a matter of fact most did not go to the Rockies to become wealthy but they ended up rich. Not rich in material wealth but rich in the feeling of freedom. They were rich in seeing a land that most would never see. They were free to come and go as they please and they were full of wanderlust, the need to see what is over the next mountain. They did as they pleased and answered to no man. This was their wealth.

The mountain man was a special breed of man and to be successful he had to be one tough hombre willing to endure all kinds of hardships; below zero cold, starvation, Indians, endless hours of hard work, and trying to keep from getting eaten by the animals most notably, the Grizzly bear. Some trappers spent weeks without seeing another white man so loneliness was an issue to overcome. Many trapped with another trapper or with several. The numbers offered a little more protection from the dreaded Blackfoot Indians that hated them for invading their land and killing the game.

In this book, for simplicity in reading, I have decided to have Shakespeare speak in normal English. In the previous books in the Tye Watkins series I had Shakespeare (Buff) speaking a different language than anyone else. The mountain man had a special jargon of their own and unless you were another trapper you would have a hard time understanding what was being said. Below are two actual conversations between trapper Louy Simmonds and John Hatcher in their jargon and then translated into normal English.

This coon has raised har so often sence he keers fur nothing now. Mind the time we tuk Pawnee topknots away to the Platte, Hatcher.

TRANSLATION: I have scalped so many Indians that nothing bothers me anymore. Do you remember the time, Hatcher, that we scalped the Pawnees near the Platte River.

Hatcher explaining why he gets up early, even in the coldest weather.

This hos is no bar to stick his nose under all the robes and lay around camp.

TRANSLATION: I am not a bear which likes to hibernate all winter.

PREFACE

    Shakespeare McDovitt began trapping beaver in the Rockies in 1815. He survived hardships and dangers for over twenty years. In 1823 he teamed up with Jim Bridger and Jerome Absher and had a great year trapping beaver, and they trapped together for years

    The first mountain man rendezvous was held in July of 1825 on Henry's Fork of the Green River. A few dozen of the mountain men gathered to sell and trade their beaver plews (skins) to the traders who had come all the way from St. Louis. It was the beginning of the annual rendezvous that lasted until the 1840's when the demand for beaver ceased. In the following years after the first rendezvous, as many as 400 trappers and sometimes as many as a 1000 friendly Indians gathered for the event.

    It was at this first rendezvous that Shakespeare and Bridger became acquainted with the youngster, Ben Watkins. Ben joined their party even though he knew nothing about trapping beaver. Shakespeare became his mentor and that started a friendship that lasted until Ben was killed in Texas by Apaches over thirty years later. During Ben's time in the mountains he became known as a 'man to ride the river with,' which meant he could be depended on when things got rough. He had a reputation with the Blackfoot and the Utes as a man to be respected as a warrior. He was even written about in some of the dime novels.

    When they quit trapping in 1836 each of the friends went their own way. Ben had went to Texas where he met and married a lady named Lori and settled just a little distance from the Rio Grande River. They had a son in 1839 and named him Tye. From the time the youngster could walk, Ben taught him to track, hunt, shoot, and when he was older, to fight with fist, gun, knife, and tomahawk. Over the years Tye honed these skills to where he was considered one of the best scouts in Texas. He was feared by the bandits and respected as a great warrior by the Apache.

Shakespeare had heard stories about this young scout in Texas from soldiers that had been stationed at Fort Clark before coming to where Shakespeare scouted in Colorado. The scout's name was Watkins. Shakespeare heard this scout's father had been a well known mountain man. He figured there was a good chance this scout was Ben's son, so at the age of seventy-one, Shakespeare made his way to Fort Clark, Texas to find out. If the man was his friend's son, he knew Ben probably had not changed and he never was one to talk about things he had accomplished. He intended to tell this scout named Tye, just what a 'real man' and friend Ben was.

His stories were interrupted by the usual problems in this country; either bandits or Apaches. This particular time was not Apaches but a gang of cutthroats that began preying on the settlers that were trying to make a life for their families along the Border. Tye was given orders to track them down and put an end to the problem. This proved to be harder and more dangerous than he or the Army could ever have imagined.

Acknowledgements

I would like to thank Ronnie Humphreys, of my home town of Levelland, Texas and Sonja Shell of Fort Clark , Texas for their time and effort in editing *Back To The Rockies*.

Fort Clark: The Lonely Sentinel   *Caleb PirtleIII*
and Michael F.Cusack

Historical Facts on the American & Canadian Fur Trade   *O. Neil Eldins*

HISTORICAL NOTE

I have tried to make this book as close to factual as possible as far as what the mountain man was, what he did, and what he endured. Hours have been spent reading material about these men that braved the dangers of the Rockies. Of course I have taken certain fictional liberties to hopefully make this book an enjoyable and exciting read.

Please enjoy 'Back to the Rockies.'

Chapter One

The sun shining the morning of April 8th, 1869 promised a beautiful day and any other time it probably would have been. Today, fourteen soldiers, including Tye's good friend Lieutenant Garrison, were to be buried in the Fort Clark cemetery. The men's lives ended in the battle against the Apache led by the warrior, Ke-ah two days earlier. Later, Ke-ah had been killed by Tye and the Apache trouble was over…for awhile at least.

Tye, sitting at the table in his and Rebecca's home, was drinking coffee and talking to his friend, Shakespeare McDovitt. Shakespeare, or Buff as he liked to be called, was an old mountain man, one of the few original ones that were still alive. His best friend back in those days was Ben Watkins, Tye's father.

Since Buff had come to the fort to meet his old friend's son, he had lived with Tye and Rebecca and he had become sort of a celebrity on the fort. All the men had heard or read stories about

1

the mountain men, but none had actually ever met one…till now, and they had a million questions for the old trapper. They also had learned what stories he had told, no matter how far-fetched, were probably true. Buff proved to them on several patrols he had scouted, that at seventy-one he could still hold his own in fights. No one doubted that he was not a man to tangle with in a fight when he was thirty-five or so years younger.

For the most part, Buff had spent what idle time they had telling stories to Tye about his pa and those days trapping beaver in the 'Shining Mountains.' He had begun trapping in 1815 and his last year was 1836 when the demand for beaver fell off. The first annual rendezvous of the mountain men was held on Henry's Fork of the Green River. This is where Buff met the strapping young man named Ben Watkins and began an unlikely friendship that would last a lifetime.

Rebecca walked into the room. "We had better start getting dressed for the services."

"See you two in a few minutes," Buff said, heading to his room to get ready. When Tye and Rebecca came out of their room they found Buff sitting on the porch decked out in black pants, white shirt and black coat. His mostly silver hair was washed, brushed, and perfectly straight, not a hair out of place. He had even shaved. This was the first time Tye or Rebecca had seen his face without the whiskers. He looked entirely different, much younger than his 70 plus years.

"My, aren't you the handsome one," Rebecca commented smiling, then kissed him on the cheek. Buff, embarrassed, stepped back and gently massaged the spot with his fingers.

"I might not have recognized you anywhere else," Tye said, slapping him on the back. Tye sighed, took a couple of steps and said, "Let's go to the services." He wanted the burial ceremony over with quickly. Lieutenant Garrison had been his friend for over a year and he wasn't looking forward to saying a final goodbye to him and the other soldiers he had led on patrol so many times.

Two long hours later, it was over. They went to Senior Master Sergeant O'Malley's home for refreshments and to visit. Sergeant O'Malley was Rebecca's father's brother. Her father and mother had been killed two years earlier by a raiding Comanche war party up north of Fort Clark a hundred or so miles. She had come to live with the O'Malley's and had met Tye, who was the Chief of Scouts at Clark. He was the best looking man she had ever seen. O'Malley told her stories about Tye and what a fine man he was. She quickly found herself falling in love with him.

Later, Post Commander James Thurston and Captain McClellan dropped by the O'Malley's to reminisce and tell

3

stories about Lieutenant Garrison. The stories were mostly about some of the funny things Garrison had said or done when he first arrived at Clark fresh out of the Point, including Buff's assessment of the lieutenant the first time he met him. They all got a big laugh remembering Buff saying, "This heer Lootenant is greener than green. He don't kno nuthin abut nuthin."

Later, after arriving back at their house an emotionally spent, Tye said he was going to lie down for awhile. He had controlled his emotions during the service and at the O'Malley's, outwardly anyway, but was drained mentally. He believed what he had heard was true in that it was tougher to keep things inside than to just let ones emotions go.

"Honey, why don't you wake me up in a couple hours," He said.

Rebecca kissed him on the cheek. "I'll get you up just before dinner is ready." She went outside and sat down on the porch beside Buff. "Today was tough on Tye," she said.

"Sho nuff," Buff answered. "He thought a lot uf that thar Lootenant Garrison and the uthers but he also killed his old frend, Ke-ah. That's a lot to handle all at once for any man. I know a lot abut lusing frens over tha yeers but I kan't imagine how it would feel killing wun." He stood up and said. "I think I'll take a walk before supper. Be back in about an hour." He stepped off the porch and walked along the bank of Los Moras Creek that wound its way through the fort.

Walking the creek reminded him of other creeks that he had walked along with his friend Ben forty years or so ago. He was remembering the many good times, and the bad, they had in the Rockies with Jim Bridger, Jerome Absher, and some of the other trappers. God, how he missed those days trapping during what was called the 'shining times' in the Rockies and the Yellowstone.

If he could go back to those days he would in a second. He had said before that if God would allow him to go back, even for a week, he would trade the years he had left on earth for the opportunity. He sat down and leaned against an oak tree and looking west, stared at the beautiful sunset. He thought this Texas sky looked just like the sky he remembered in the Rockies.

He was glad he had come to Fort Clark to meet his old friend's son. He regretted he had not come before to see Ben. Ben had been killed several years earlier and Buff's not seeing him was one of the two regrets in his life. The other was not seeing his parents, brothers, or sisters since he left home to be a mountain man. That was fifty four years ago and he didn't know if he still had family living or not.

He was content living with Tye and Rebecca and was elated that at his age he had been able to help Tye on patrols. He was almost as happy as Tye was when he heard about Rebecca being pregnant. He felt for the first time in over fifty years that he was part of a family and he loved it. He laughed thinking that he had never been married and was maybe fixing to be a grandpa.

Sitting under the oak he thought of his friends he had trapped with that were dead. Joseph Dij Bijeau was reported killed but no one ever found where he was buried. Jedediah Smith was the most educated and religious trapper he had known. He was killed by Comanche warriors in 1831. Hugh Glass who survived a mauling by a grizzly and was left for dead by his friends. Badly mauled and with a broken leg, he crawled and limped a hundred miles to the Cheyenne River and on a raft he built, floated to Fort Kiowa. It was one of the most amazing feats of survival in history. He survived that only to die at the hands of hostile Arikara Indians in 1833. There were many other men he had trapped with that all died from Indians or the one thing the mountain man feared most...the grizzly. There was Jim Baker who was still alive the last time he heard and of course, his long time friend and partner, Jim Bridger who he knew was still alive.

Of all these men, Ben Watkins was his closest friend. He would never have guessed it would have been that way because of their first meeting at the 1825 rendezvous in the Green river Country.

He looked at the setting sun again and shut his eyes and relaxed. He let his mind drift let back to those days so long ago in the beautiful Rocky Mountains. He saw Bridger, and Ben, and he remembered…remembering…dreaming.

He woke up suddenly as a hand was shaking his shoulder. He was startled to see Tye standing above him.

"Taking you a nap old timer?" he asked laughing.

"Guess so," Buff answered, slightly embarrassed.

"Supper's waiting," Tye said as he walked back toward his house. Buff stood up and followed him into the house.

"You okay, Buff?" Rebecca asked. "We got a little worried about you. It's not like you to be late for a meal," she added laughing. "You two sit down and I'll set the table.

"What were you doing?" Tye asked.

"Nuthin much, jus remembering thangs."

"Such as."

"I wus thanking abut tha old days and yur pa, Bridger, and me. I wus thanking abut all tha frens I had lost over tha yeers. I guess tha burial today uf thos boys got me to thanking. I wus thanking abut how nice it wus now havin yu and Rebecca as frens,"

"Not just friends Buff," Rebecca said as she placed plates of food in front of him and Tye. "You are part of our family and always will be."

Buff swallowed the lump in his throat. "I kno that and yu two jus don't reelize how much tha meens to an old man like me."

"You're only as old as you feel Buff. I hope I am as active and healthy as you when I pass seventy years.

Buff nodded. "The good Lord has blessed me, not doubt about that." Rebecca sat down with her plate and they begin eating.

"Buff," Tye said suddenly. "You have told stories about you and pa but," he looked Buff in the eyes. "I want to know everything about him. I want to know every detail of you two's life together."

"Now?" Buff questioned.

"You have anything better to do," Tye said smiling.

"Everything?"

"Every last detail that you can remember," Tye said. "Tell me everything from the first time you met until the last time you saw each other. I've got to know about my pa's life before he settled down and married Ma. He told me a few stories but I want to know everything in between."

Buff leaned back in his chair. "Gonna take awhile," he said.

Rebecca stood up. "I'll get you two a drink."

A minute later she appeared and handed each man a cup of whiskey. Buff leaned back in his chair, took a sip, and began talking.

Gary McMillan

Chapter Two

"It was a warm July 1st, 1825 and I was enjoying lying in the tallgrass and listening to all the shouting and celebrating that was going on all around me. This was the first of many rendezvous in the coming years of the mountain men. They would be held each summer and this first one was on Henry's Fork of the Green River." "I had begun my life as a trapper seven years earlier and until the last two years had damn neared starved to death, froze to death, barely escaped death several times from the Blackfoot, and once, was almost killed by a dead buffalo."

"A dead buffalo?" Rebecca said with a quizzical look on her face.

Buff laughed. "It seems this buffalo I had shot wasn't dead and when I stuck my skinning knife in tha soft belly of tha cow she came to life and damn near trampled me to death before she fell over dead. I guess it was a pretty funny sight to those watching, but not so for me. My name, Shakespeare McDovitt,

11

was changed that day. My friend and partner, Jim Bridger, from that day forward called me Buff, short for buffalo, and the handle has stayed with me since."

"Before I go any farther let me say this about the trappers. Tye, I know you are good at what you do and you could probably have been a very successful trapper or as the novelist say, a mountain man. There is probably nothing on earth as beautiful as the Rockies in the summer with the green hills and the tall mountains capped with snow. The willows, cottonwoods, and countless forms of green vegetation line the banks of the rivers and creeks in the lowlands; the beautiful aspen and pines growing thick on the higher regions. Whitetail deer in the lower lands; the blacktail along with the shaggy buffalo roamed the highlands. Bear, wolves, squirrels, chipmunks, and large number of rabbits and other varmints were everywhere."

"When I was sixteen, an old man came by our home and spent the night. He had been in the Rockies for years trapping. He spent several hours telling my pa about things he had saw and experienced. Of course I was listening, taking it all in. From that night on, that was my dream until one day I told my parents. I was nineteen years old when I told them I wanted to go to the Rockies and be a trapper. My mother almost had a heart attack and my pa thought I had lost my mind. I had my mind made up and intended to be gone only for a couple years. I was going to come back a rich man and help my family." He shook his head. "I never made it back. Those mountains got hold of me and would not let go. It was not exactly as that old man had said, at least for a couple years. It was beautiful alright, but to be a successful trapper entailed a little more than showing up with traps."

"Even the hardiest who tried trapping had a hard time. You had to love it or you would never make it even one winter. It was a place where you were on your own…no doctors, no wives to nurse you back to health if you became sick or injured. It was a place where a simple broken leg in the winter could be a death sentence. It was an every day struggle to survive the below zero winters with their brutal blizzards, the grizzlies and wolves that would take a careless man as a meal anytime, and of course the Blackfoot, Utes, and other tribes that resented us coming into their land and killing their game. For those of us who loved that way of life, the reward was significant though…complete and total freedom."

"Tell me about the Blackfeet, Buff," Tye said. "Are they similar to the Apache?"

Buff nodded. "All the different tribes I have met, lived with, or fought are all similar. They are a proud people and will fiercely defend their land and families from an enemy and

13

anyone that is not of their tribe is considered one. If they feel you wronged them or lied to them you are in serious trouble. They would never steal from anyone in their tribe but they may steal your pants just for the enjoyment of proving they could. They are terrific warriors and are fearless in battle just like your Apaches are here." He paused for a second considering what he would say about the Blackfeet.

"The Blackfoot Confederacy consisted of the North Piegan, the South Piegan, the Kainai or Blood, and the Siksika Nations. Together they called themselves the *'Niitsitapii'* (the Real People). They all shared a common language and culture. They ranged from the Rocky Mountains all the way up into Canada. Blackfoot bands consisted for the most part from ten to thirty or so lodges which meant from eighty to over two hundred people which, from what I have seen here, made their bands a little larger than most Apache bands. They, like all tribes, moved frequently following the game, especially the buffalo. The buffalo was revered and regarded as a Medicine Animal by the Blackfoot. Their skulls were placed outside their Medicine Lodges and a white buffalo was sacred."

"How did they get the name Blackfoot," Rebecca asked while putting up the dishes.

"Well, their feet were not black," Buff said chuckling. "Their name came from their moccasins, Rebecca. They died them

14

black. They were just Indians doing what they had to do to preserve their way of life just like the Kiowa, Sioux, Comanche, and the Apache are doing. We did not hate them for their killing our friends; they were, like your Apaches here, just trying to survive and we were intruding on what they thought was their land...forcing them out. If I was an Injun, I would do the same thing."

"Now, saying that, let's get back to the story telling. Like I said, this here rendezvous was the first time us trappers had an opportunity to sell and trade our pelts to fur company representatives who were present. Before, we had to make the trek out of the mountains to the trading post to trade and sell our furs. This year, I and the rest got top price for the beaver pelts with them bringing three dollars a pound. This was good money, but there was a catch. The supplies we needed were brought also by the fur company representatives, but the prices were extremely high. Cloth for example, was as high as ten dollars a yard; in St Louis, the same cloth was fifty to ninety cents a yard. Staples like sugar and coffee sold for two dollars per pound verses fifteen cents in St Louis. It was the same for lead, powder, and every other item we needed to survive. It was the age old story of supply and demand and as the years went by, the prices kept going up. The trappers could travel two hundred miles or so to buy their supplies and get a much better deal on

15

them, but by the time they returned to the mountains, they would lose two months or more."

"I was satisfied with my dealing with the traders. I had my food staples of sugar, flour, beans, coffee, salt, powder, lead, a new skinning knife, four new traps, and just about every other thing I needed. I had a little over two hundred dollars left in cash. The money and supplies was what I had to show for a year's work and I was as happy as a man could be. I, like most of the other trappers, was not expecting to get rich trapping beaver. Our riches was seeing what was over the other side of the mountain, the freedom to do as we please, seeing the beautiful Rockies, feeling the excitement and the danger, and seeing things no other white man had seen before."

"This was a great year compared to the previous years for me. Bridger, Jerome Absher, and I had teamed up, and with our helping each other did well. Most of the trappers did pretty well, and of course, the traders were extremely pleased."

"The rendezvous, besides being a time for the trappers to sell their goods, was a time for drinking, bragging, wrestling, bare knuckle fighting, shooting contest and horse racing. It was this day, this first day of July, that Bridger and me watched this young whippersnapper whip several men that were older than he was in wrestling and bare knuckle fighting."

One man, embarrassed by losing to this youngster, recruited two other trappers to teach him a 'lesson.' They caught the young man away from camp and jumped him. Jim and me were watching and were amazed the kid was handling the three men pretty well. After watching for a minute we waded in and Jim cold cocked one with his rifle butt and I did the same to another. The teenager took care of the third and was upset that we had stepped in and spoiled his fun. "

"After calming the youngster down, the three of us sat around talking. This kid, Ben Watkins, was big, maybe two inches over six foot tall and close to two hundred pounds. He had black hair that hung to his shoulders, a scraggly excuse for a mustache and the bluest eyes a man could ever hope to see. He was also a good looking man that was thick through the shoulders and chest and then tapered to a narrow waist and hips."

"Jim took an instant liking to the youngster because of his spunk. After talking with him for a few minutes, I saw only a young man that was green as they come as far as being a trapper was concerned. He knew absolutely nothing about the mountains or trapping beaver, or anything else about being in the wilderness. I even wondered how he found his way to the rendezvous."

"Like I said though, old Bridger liked him right off, and even though I didn't think it was a good idea, he invited this greener to join our trapping party. A week later, our group and other trappers left to start preparing for the fall trapping season. I was somehow appointed this here young man's mentor. Like I said, he didn't know nothing about nothing, but I soon found out he was a quick learner. He was smart and you only had to tell him once the how's and why's of doing something. He asked a lot of questions...good questions that a man would want to know if he was going to make it out here and for some reason, I began to like him."

"Like I said he was a quick learner, and by the time the fall trapping season came around he was ready to start trapping beaver. He only had four traps, so I loaned him two of mine."

"Sitting around the campfire the night before we set our first traps, I was telling him more things he needed to know."

"Take your stake and drive it into the bottom of the pond good and solid. After the stake is secure attach the chain that is on the trap to it. The stake has to be solid because some of these beavers can weigh more than fifty pounds. Make sure the stake is far enough from the bank that the beaver can't haul himself and the trap on land. If he does he can sometimes chew his foot off and get plum away. The object is to set your stake to where the beaver will be kept in the water and drown. Put a couple of good drops of the scent around to attract the critter."

"The scent, or what us trappers call medicine, is a mixture of fluid from their scent gland that is at the base of their tail, plus a concoction we mix up. Some trappers don't use anything but the liquid from scent glands, but we do it a little different. We take nutmeg, cloves, and cinnamon, and pulverize it and mix it with the liquid from the glands. It ends up a thick liquid that old beavers just can't resist coming to. All the time I was talking, the kid never took his eyes off me. I could tell he was listening well."

"How many beavers can one expect to trap in the fall and spring seasons?" he asked.

"I thought for a minute. Maybe three hundred and fifty give or take a few. Four hundred is not uncommon." I heard Jed Smith had six hundred and sixty-eight this year. That has to be a record. I could see Ben's eyes widen as he did some math in his mind. "Whatever you make, the traders are going to get most of it when you buy your supplies for the next year. I had three hundred twenty five pelts this year; after buying supplies I had a little over two hundred dollars left."

"Sudden howls from nearby caused Ben's head to jerk around so quick he was lucky he didn't break his neck. Bridger and me was laughing at him, but shut up when he stood up and gave us that look we had seen when he whipped them men a few days ago. I told him it was just a few wolves hunting for supper."

He looked back in the direction the howls had come from. "Do they attack humans?"

"Old Bridger was a great one to josh people, especially pilgrims like Ben. He said, "not normally, but when they are in a pack like those are they might just eat a man who ventured out of camp or if they let the fire burn down. They are like most critters out here and are afraid of fire." He lay down and pulled his blanket up to his chin, looked at me, winked and smiled. I lay down and then had to muffle a laugh when I saw young Ben add wood to the fire and lay down after looking nervously in all directions; he also had a pistol in his hand. I knew he wasn't going to get much sleep so I told him that Bridger was just joshing him some. I laughed again when he said he knew that."

"I decided during the night, that this first day I would not set my traps but would help Ben put his where they would do some good. We were walking the creek just as the sky was turning gray. It would not be full light for a couple hours because it was always late morning before the sun was high enough to be above the tops of the mountains. I explained what to look for. "Look for pools formed by the dams the beavers has built. Sometimes you will see fresh cut trees they have gnawed down to start a dam."

"Two hours later we were back in camp, having put out all six traps. We would run them again late in the afternoon. If we had beaver, we would re-bait the holes and then run them again at first light. I explained to him that if we were finding beaver, we would stay busy from daylight to well after dark. After running the traps in the morning and re-baiting the traps, he would spend the rest of the day skinning and fleshing the plews. He then had to stretch them out on willow hoops to dry before running the traps late in the evening and maybe skinning and fleshing plews by firelight till time to hit the sack."

"His first day he had four beavers and I showed him how to skin and flesh the plews. I showed him how to stretch the pelts on green willow hoops to dry. He paid attention and I only had to tell him how to do things one time. I cooked some beaver tail that night and he thought it was as good as anything he had ever eaten."

"We spent a week on this part of the creek and took a total of sixty-one beaver. We decided it was time to move farther up stream. This day would be the day Jim, Absher, and I found out exactly what we had for a partner."

Late that afternoon, we set up camp on a small island in the creek. There was a lot of driftwood, some being whole trees, on the island which proved to be a life saver later. The water was a little over knee deep all around the island. After camp was set up, we were startled by seeing nine or ten Blackfoot warriors come out of the aspens and charging our camp, screaming like demons from hell and releasing their arrows. One of the flint tipped arrows caught me in the left shoulder. We scrambled for our rifles and each of us got one shot and three of them devils went to the happy hunting ground. There wasn't even time to pull our pistols before the remaining warriors came out of the water on our little island. Ben jumped up screaming like a crazy person, which I think startled the Blackfoot just for a second and then they were on Ben, who stood there swinging a tomahawk in his right hand and slashing with his butcher knife in his left, still screaming all the while."

"I don't know exactly what happened with him next because I sorta got busy myself. The fight lasted less than thirty seconds, but like all Injun fights, seemed like forever. The three warriors left standing were running like the devil was after them when Ben pulled his pistol and shot one square through the shoulder blades. Absher, who had been away from camp showed up, and shot one as they reached the far bank. Bridger looked at Ben, then at me and smiled. Ben had shot one when they charged, killed three in hand to hand fighting, and killed a fourth as they tried to escape. That was when we learned we had a partner that had 'the hair of the bear' which is about the highest praise a mountain man could give for another man."

"We broke camp and left to go farther upstream as we figure those dead boys friends would come looking for us as soon as the one that got away could lead them back. Bridger broke the shaft off the arrow in my shoulder, but we had to get away so doctoring it would have to wait. We stayed in the stream for almost a mile to keep our tracks from the Blackfoot. It was full dark when we got out of the water where we found a rocky bank and hopefully, we would leave no sign of our leaving the creek. We traveled another five miles parallel to the creek, but stayed a couple hundred yards in the woods. Our tracks would not be easy to follow. Travel was slow and when we finally stopped, it was almost four in the morning. I don't mind telling you it was the most miserable few hours of my life. My shoulder was hurting something fierce. Bridger insisted Ben get the shaft out because he needed to learn because chances were, it would not be the last time. Ben, after arguing that he couldn't, did a right nice job of getting the shaft out of my shoulder. Bridger, cackling like an old woman, poured whiskey into the hole that burned like the fires of hell. They set up camp while I rested some. That damn shoulder was hurting something fierce. We decided to have one man awake during the day and that night to watch for the devils. We slept with a pistol in our hand and our rifle handy."

Chapter Three

"Near as we could figure, we were camped on a small creek that came out of Bear Lake. I was plum laid up with that shoulder and if I moved much it would start paining me pretty good.. Old Ben proved just what a friend he was going to be. He set and ran his traps as well as doing the same for me. There were a lot of beaver and by the end of the first week, the four of us had near a hundred plews. I helped some after the first couple days, but Ben worked his tail off running mine and his traps, skinning and fleshing the beavers."

"Old Stumpy, that's the name given to Absher by Bridger, had the best week of any of us as he had thirty-one plews." Buff laughed, stopped his story and took another sip of whiskey before continuing. "Old Bridger had a knack for attaching nick names to people like I told you before when he named me Buff. Absher was six feet tall and skinny as a rail, so naturally, Bridger gave him the name of Stumpy. He used to say old Stump would never be killed by the Injuns because he was so

25

damn skinny they would never be able to hit him with their arrows. Stumpy was frail looking, but I'm telling you one thing, he was a man one could depend on it a fight. He was meaner than a old she bear with cubs in one and never backed down. The only draw back was his talking. He talked all the time, never shut up. He said it was a family trait, this talking. It was a minor thing, so we over looked it because of all the positive things from having him as a friend and a partner."

"We moved camp again after a week of trapping. We left a few beavers so they could reproduce. This not trapping a creek completely out was not shared by all the trappers in the mountains. We had done pretty well so far. We had close to one hundred and sixty plews between us. I had the fewest, but at least I had some, thanks to Ben."

"We stayed on the same creek and camped four miles up from our last camp. My shoulder was getting better every day. I could move it some without a lot of pain, but lifting anything heavy was out of the question. Sitting by the small fire that night, we were talking about different things, when the discussion about old Ephraim came up. Ephraim was the name us trappers gave the grizzly bear. Most of us trappers feared him more than the Blackfoot. He was the most unpredictable creature on earth. If you stumbled upon one, he might look you over and go on his way, or he might charge you without hesitation. Ben was all ears as he was not familiar with the grizzly bear and his ways, and chances were he would meet one someday."

"Bridger was doing the most talking because he had had survived several encounters with Ephraim. He said they would sometimes charge like they were going to tear you apart and then stop, sniff, look around, and then amble off like you were not even there. The next time, they might not stop and things could get serious in a hurry. It was almost impossible to stop a grizzly with one shot, and generally, being wounded only made them madder. He said the best thing, besides avoiding them, was to stand your ground and yell as loud as you could. Sometimes this would scare them off, sometime it wouldn't and then you were in for a fight. Never run he said, as they would quickly overtake you. On level ground, a grizzly can run as fast as a galloping horse for a short period. Never, he said, get around a mother with cubs and for sure, never get between them. She will attack you without provocation to protect her cubs."

"Ben was curious and asked what he was to do if attacked. Bridger laughed, just get ready to meet your maker son, he said and laughed again. Little did we know that in a couple days, Ben would find out himself what it was like to encounter the most fearsome of God's creatures. As I looked back on it, I realized it was the first time we had even discussed the grizzly.

Then, two days later, Ben meets one. I always thought that was kind of strange. The Lord sometimes works in strange ways because without that conversation, Ben just might not have survived his meeting the 'Lord of the Mountains.'"

"The creek was stocked plum full of beaver. By the end of the first day, we had twenty plews stretched on the willow hoops drying. We were excited as it looked like we were in for a great year. After running our traps the next morning, we were all talking, as each of us had four more plews and could not wait till we ran them again later in the evening. That was when Ben met his grizzly."

"Ben was trapping closest to camp and Bridger was a mile further up the creek. Stumpy and me were trapping down the creek. Ben was bent over taking a beaver from his trap when he said he sensed danger. He slowly raised his head and moving only his eyes searched the far bank. He saw nothing and as he was turning his head to look behind him he heard the growl and immediately knew what it was. He turned and was face to face with a grizzly that was standing on his hind legs and looked to be about nine foot tall.

Twenty feet separated them, as both man and bear stared at each other. The bear was moving his head back and forth sniffing the air. Ben was looking at the huge teeth in the bears gaping mouth and the four inch claws. He could imagine what they would do to a man with one swipe. He looked at the bear and then at his rifle which was six or seven feet away. He was undecided what to do; try to outrun him, but Bridger had said that was not a good idea, or make a try for his rifle. He decided on the latter and yelled as loud as he could before he dove for the rifle. In the instant before he dove for the gun, he saw the hesitation of the bear when he yelled. It gave him enough time to grab his Hawken rifle and cock it all in one motion. The grizzly dropped to all fours and letting out a deafening roar, charged.

Ben quickly sighted down the barrel and squeezed the trigger. There was a flash and the Hawken bucked against his shoulder. It was a lucky shot as the .53 caliber ball struck the bear right between the eyes and dropped him in his tracks. Ben could not believe it. His hands were shaking and his legs felt like mush as he stared at the monster. Out of habit he re-loaded the Hawken after taking a deep breath and relaxing a little so his hands were steady again."

"The bear suddenly came alive... and he was mad, killing mad. Ben's shot to the bear's thick skull had only stunned him and he was coming after this thing that had hurt him. He stood on his hind legs and waved those tremendous paws with the four inch claws in the air. Ben aimed again and shot the bear in the center of the chest. The bear stumbled backwards a couple steps then dropped to all fours and came again. Ben pulled his pistol and shot into the bears head. The bear stopped, shook his head and charged again. Ben picked up the beaver and tossed it at the bear hoping he would take the beaver and leave. The bear slapped the forty pound beaver with his paw and the animal was propelled through the air like a man would throw a rock. Ben pulled his Bowie and prepared to meet the grizzly with the only weapon he had left."

"He knew he was going to get hurt, and hurt bad, but what choice did he have. The bear hit him with a paw that knocked him about ten feet farther into the creek. The bear stood up,and Ben looking up at this tremendous creature, figured the last thing he would see on this earth was those tremendous jaws just before they clamped around his head. Ben had the knife in his hand and had it drawn back to drive it into the bear when he heard two shots, watched the bear stagger, and then fall into the water."

Dazed and not really knowing what happened, he sat down not even feeling the frigid water he was in. Then hands were pulling him up, helping him out of the water and onto the bank. He stared at Bridger in front of him, but really didn't recognize him. Bridger and I helped him to camp and Stumpy had come running in about that time. He thought it was Indians from all the shooting. I quickly explained to him what happened and he looked at the bear in the water, then at Ben. Bridger brought some whiskey and gave Ben a good belt of it."

"It worked. Ben blinked a few times and gradually began getting his senses back. We laughed when he yelled "Grizzly." Bridger went to his saddle bags and came back with a needle and thread. Ben had a bad cut on his shoulder and the side of his neck where the claws dug in. It was a good thing his shoulder took most of the force of the blow, otherwise, he would have had a broken neck. After some cussing from Ben, who never cursed, when I poured the whiskey on the wounds; Bridger sewed his cuts up. After Jim finished, Ben was shaking some, so we put my buffalo robe on him and let him lie next to the fire."

"After making sure Ben was okay, we left to finish running our traps. Bridger came back with seven, three of which was from Ben's traps. Before we skinned them we decided to get the bear from the water. The three of us struggled, but finally got the dead bear on the bank. After skinning him and fleshing the pelt, we stretched the hide so it would dry. It would make a fine blanket for Ben. We cut some of the meat and roasted it over the fire. We also had several pounds of meat that we could carry with us. This time of the year meat would keep because of the cold nights and cool days."

"The next two days passed quickly with Bridger, Absher, and me taking turns running Ben's traps. We woke up the

31

morning of the third day and were surprised to find Ben already up and the coffee boiling. He was feeling much better and said he was as hungry as a she wolf with pups, which as you know, is pretty hungry. While drinking coffee, chewing a biscuit with hot bacon, he told us how much he appreciated us running his traps. There was a lot of beaver and we had taken twenty three of those critters from his traps and skinned them for him. He said he thought he would be able to handle the traps today."

"That day was pretty much the same as the previous days; bait traps, run them and take beaver out, re-bait them, skin the ones you caught, run the traps again, take the beaver out, skin them, and then hit the blankets for a few hours. Like I told you before, trapping beaver wasn't easy, but if one was willing to work, he could make a decent living. Jim thought this would be our last day before moving. We brought our traps in just before dark, along with our catch of beaver. It had been a great week of trapping, but we would move up the creek a few miles in the morning. Jim was against trapping out an area. He always wanted to leave a few beaver, so they could make babies and the area would be good again in a couple years."

Chapter Four

"We stopped after traveling about five or six miles up the creek. Ben, Stumpy, and me set up camp while Jim explored farther up the creek. We had camp set up and a small fire going, when Jim returned, just before dark. He told us, we were only three miles or so from Bear Lake, and there was a hell of lot of beaver between here and the lake. This was news that we wanted to hear and everyone was in good spirits. We discussed our plans for the next day while our bear steaks cooked over the small fire of dead wood which was surrounded by rocks. There was no sense letting anyone know where we were, just because we were hungry. Many a trapper had been killed because they advertised their whereabouts by using green wood that gave off a lot of smoke or by not making small fires whose glowing flames were shielded from prying eyes by the rocks placed around it."

"I remember that night because of the conversation. Old Bridger got off on one of his tales about Indian myths that young

Ben soaked up like desert sand that ain't seen any rain for months." He chuckled, remembering one of the tales before he spoke again. "Seems like there was a mysterious animal that walked like a man, was almost eight feet tall, hairy, and very strong. His footprints were almost a foot and a half long and 10 inches wide and when walking, his stride was almost four feet."

"Now, young Ben was taking this all in. He said he had never heard of such an animal. It was all me and Absher could do to keep from laughing out loud. Jim, seeing that Ben was hooked, really stepped up his story. This here creature was known to carry off full grown warriors, one on each shoulder, as if they weighed nothing and they were never seen again...not even their bones. This had gone on as long as some of the old men of the tribes could remember. Never once was the animal caught, and there was never more than one seen at a time, leading most to believe there was only one of them, and he was very, very old. He was thought to be one of the remaining ancients, that lived long ago, whose images could be found on the walls in caves. Among the trappers, some wondered if this is what happened to some of their friends that disappeared over the years and were never heard from again. I know one trapper that actually saw the creature from a distance. He said it reminded him of a bear that walked upright. He was scared as hell, even

34

when he told us about it a few days later. That old demon is still out there…waiting, and watching."

Buff slapped his leg again, hee-hawed loudly and then, regaining his composure, continued. "You should have seen young Ben. He just sat there, didn't move, his mouth open and eyes big as saucers. I got up and started to walk away when he asked me where I was going. I told him I had to answer nature's call." Shakespeare slapped his leg again and hee-hawed loudly and then regaining his composure continued. "He told me to be careful and then asked me if I wanted him to come with me." Buff laughed again. "Actually, I just had to get away before I busted a gut laughing."

"I can't believe pa would believe such as a story." Tye said, rubbing the back of his neck and shaking his head in disbelief.

"Tye, in those days there was a lot of things us white men didn't understand. We found out that a lot of the old Indian lore actually had some truth to them. There was a certain fear…no that's not the proper word… not fear…maybe uneasiness that set in when a man went into a country no white man had seen before. When it was dark and the wind was rustling the leaves of the aspen and singing through the tall pines, the wolves howling mixing with the other night sounds, certain things could run through a man's mind at that time…things that made a man have daunting thoughts. A man alone can conjure up all sorts of images in his mind that he actually believes he saw. Anyway, old Bridger had a knack for words and that's one reason he was so well known. He was a first class trapper, but so were a lot of others that no one heard about. He was a tall tale telling sonofagun, and he could make things believable."

He paused for a moment gathering his thought again. "It was early September now, and the night time temperature was dropping with every passing day. We trapped the creek for a little over a week and each of us had a passel of beaver plews. For a change, nothing out of the ordinary had happened. We saw a few deer, a couple grizzly, varmints' of all kinds, but no two legged ones. We broke camp the next morning and made our way along the bank of Bear Lake looking for another creek that we could trap. We figured we had two weeks of trapping left and then we would find a place to hole up for the winter. Now was the time to get the best plews because the beaver were putting on their thick winter fur."

"We found a creek and made our way down it for three or four miles. There were signs of a lot of beaver living in the creek and we figured we would end the season here and with a lot of new plews."

We had a great ten days of trapping and each of us had almost more plews than his pack animal could carry. It was a great year. Our little group had done well, and I had a friend that would mean everything to me for the rest of my life."

It was time to find a place to hole up for the winter. We found a cave on the south side of a cliff that was over fifty foot deep. Being on the south side the cold winter winds would not blow directly into it and the rain and snow would be kept on the slopes. Ben shot a mountain buffalo and I killed a huge elk that first day. We spent the next week hunting and bringing meat into the cave. It was dropping below freezing at night and warming to no more than forty or fifty degrees during the daytime making it possible to keep the meat from spoiling. We spent two whole days doing nothing but bringing in firewood. We had plenty of grass from the creek for the horses. We had a camp that we felt was going to be the best any of us had ever had to ride out the brutal winter of the Rockies. Little did we know just how lucky we were to find this cave."

"That winter of 1826 was brutal. The sun didn't shine for days and days, snow that fell continuously, and the temperature never got above freezing. At night, we would see temperatures from below zero to around ten above."

A knock on the door of the cabin interrupted Buff . Tye stood up and walked to the door and opened it.

"Captain McClellan," he said stepping back. "Come in and join the party."

37

Stepping into the room McClellan removed his hat and bowed slightly to Rebecca. "You are as pretty as ever Rebecca," he said to a smiling Rebecca and then shook hands with Tye and Buff.

"What brings you over at this time of night," Tye asked the captain.

"News from southeast of here…bad news," McClellan said. Tye motioned for him to sit down.

"Make yourself comfortable, Captain and let's hear what's going on."

McClellan settled in the chair offered him and spoke. "Major Thurston had been hearing rumors about a small gang of men raising hel…." He remembered Rebecca and stopped in mid sentence. "Some men causing a lot of problems south of Fort Inge," he said slightly embarrassed by his almost use of profanity. "Apparently, the rumors were true because a young man just stumbled into the fort, half dead about an hour ago. He said that his home was attacked by four men and his parents were killed. He doesn't know about his sixteen year old sister. He was shot in the shoulder and had a bullet burn across his left temple, which had knocked him unconscious. When he regained consciousness, his home was burned and he could not find his sister. He was unable to bury his parents because of his injuries.

He rounded up an old plow horse they owned and managed to make it here.

"Where is he now?" Tye asked.

"Thurston is with him at the infirmary and wanted you to come and talk with him."

Tye stood up as did everyone else. "Let's go Captain." He turned to Rebecca and kissed her on the cheek. "I'll be back in a little while." As they started out the door he asked what the youngster's last name was.

"Jenkins I think the major said," McClellan said.

Tye stopped and turned. "This youngster about fourteen, slim, with sandy hair?"

"That pretty well describes him. Do you know them?"

Tye swore under his breath. "Lets go," he said walking out the door and then took off at a fast trot leaving a bewildered McClellan, Rebecca, and Buff.

"Wonder why he took off like that?" Rebecca asked to no one in particular.

"From the way he described that kid, and the way he left, I figure he knew them," Buff said watching Tye's back disappear in the darkness.

Gary McMillan

Chapter Five

James Baxter stood up, buttoned his pants and strapped on his gun belt. He was the last of the bunch to have his way with the young girl. She was half dead from the beating and physical assault on her body. Susan Jenkins was sixteen years old, and before the beating and assault by the four men, had been a lovely thing to look at. Now, she lay moaning with a broken nose, one eye swollen shut, bite marks on her stomach and breast, and wanting to do nothing but die. She had watched her brother shot from a distance; then watched her mother and father murdered. She was dirty, used, and felt no decent man would ever want her. 'God,' she thought. 'Just let me die.'

James walked over to the others with a big smile on his face. The others were his uncles, Bill and Robert Baxter. The fourth man was the leader of the little band of cutthroats, the half breed, Running Elk or "The Breed," as folks called him. He was a ruthless killer, called very few men friends, not even the ones he rode with now. He was half Mexican, half Apache, and all hate.

41

He killed indiscriminately, white, Indian, Mexican, man or woman, and never lost a moment's sleep over any one of them.

Bill and Robert were brothers, with Bill at forty-five, four years older than Robert. The oldest, Lester, was killed in the battle of Bull Run a few years earlier. Lester was James's father and after the war, the older brothers came home to find their nephew living alone in what remained of their home. Three months earlier, a patrol of Yankees had came through while he had been in the fields, and killed his mother and younger brother. He got a glimpse of the soldiers, but could not identify any of them except for the red stripe on their pants. He found his mother and brother in a stand of trees, shot through the head. He managed to save part of the house, which had been set on fire, bury his mother and brother, and lived there for three months until Bill and Robert showed up.

The brothers, hardened by years of fighting, showed no remorse over their loss of family and home. It seemed death and destruction had been with them forever, and was just accepted as part of life, just as light followed darkness and winter followed the summer. They took the youngster with them when they left and headed west, toward Texas, where they heard the land was free for the taking as were the men and women who settled there. The word was out there were a lot of land and only a few lawmen, which made it even more appealing to them

James was seventeen years old and ignorant of the world outside his home when Bill and Robert showed up. Running and living with his uncles the last three years had him as calloused over robbing and killing as they were. He always had a short temper and now found that he had a knack for being very quick with a gun; the combination of the two had led to some men being killed.

Bill was an inch short of six feet and thick through the shoulders and arms. He would fight at the drop of a hat and had never lost a stand-up-knock'um-down fight. He had beaten a man to death with his fist a month earlier in Louisiana and the three of them had to get out of town quick. He was the worse of the three relatives as far as being aggressive and killing when it wasn't necessary.

The younger brother, Robert, was a follower. He was laid back and just followed his older brothers lead. He was slow tempered and didn't necessarily condone the killing, but at the same time he didn't want to leave the only family he had left. He was a couple inches shorter than his brother and only weighed about a hundred and forty pounds, which was fifty less than Bill. He was much more of a thinker than Bill and he often dreamed of finding a place to settle down, and maybe even raise a family. He took a lot of ribbing whenever he brought up the subject. Settling down and actually working was far removed from the other twos way of thinking. It was much easier to let the other man work, then take what they had..

Running Elk's birth name was Miguel Espinosa. His father was Mexican and his mother was a Mescalero Apache. He was short and stocky, like all Apache, and he let his raven colored hair touch his shoulders. He wore the red head band of an Apache warrior and the clothes of a vaquero, except for the knee high Apache moccasin boots. He was a vicious killer and preferred the knife over the gun. Sticking the blade into another's belly gave him a satisfaction he did not get by simply pulling the trigger of a gun. He had no real friends and like a lot of other half-breeds felt like he belonged to no one. As a child, he was the butt of jokes by other kids because of his being a half-breed; these slurs burned inside him and slowly turned him to hating everyone. He was not above killing a white man either. Race was no barrier when it came to his hate.

James adjusted his gun belt and sat down on a dead log next to Robert. "Pretty thing ain't she," he commented. No one said anything. "What are we going to do with her?" he asked.

"What the hell do you think we are going to do," Bill replied.

"Take her with us?" James said.

"You stupid brat," Bill spit out. "Take her with us so she can maybe get away and identify us." He spit tobacco juice on the ground and more words spewed from his tobacco stained lips.

"Take her with us…brilliant idea James," he said sarcastically. "This is what we are going to do with her," he said walking over to the girl, pulled his gun and shot her in the head. The sudden shock of the killing stunned James and Robert. The Mexican just smiled and thought to himself that this gringo was like him. He might just grow to like him.

Bill casually replaced the spent cartridge, holstered his gun and walked back to the men. "She ain't saying nothing now," he said laughing and sitting back down.

"Was that really necessary, Bill?" Robert asked.

"You thinking like the brat, brother?" Bill asked spitting into the small fire.

James jumped up and instantly a gun appeared in his hand. "Don't you call me a brat again, Bill," he said sternly with the gun pointed at Bills belly.

Bill, startled by the sudden appearance of the gun smiled and said. "Sit down James, I didn't mean nothing by it." James slowly relaxed and placed the gun in the holster and sat down. Bill relaxed also, but would not forget the gun being pulled on him.

Robert tried to ignore his bullying older brother and hot tempered nephew. He was trying to piece together the events of the last twenty-four hours that led them to the killing of the girl. He felt bad for her and wasn't going to do anything to her, but

45

the other making fun of him finally led him to rape her. He felt even worse after he was through with her. His thoughts drifted back to yesterday.

They had came across the homestead last night and decided to wait until the morning, when they could scout it out to see who and how many people were there before going in. Waiting resulted in a little conflict among the four because they had been without food since the day before. Bill wanted to just charge on down and kill anyone that moved but for once he listened to someone else.

The breed spoke up. "Two years ago three companions and me attacked a small homestead without checking things out first. I was the only one to escape and I had a bullet in my side and a hole through my right calf. I found out later there was a father and three teenage sons in that house. We charged in and hit a wall of bullets. We never got within fifty yards of them and don't think we got off more than one shot each. Three men and horses went down immediately and I veered away and managed to stay in the saddle but the bullet that went through my calf went into my horse's lungs. He was game though and ran almost a mile before he went down. I learned a valuable lesson that day...don't ever under estimate anyone. It almost cost me my life."

Bill reluctantly agreed. They made camp about a mile away. They were watching at the break of dawn. The outhouse was used by a kid who went to the fields, a young girl, and finally a man, who both went back into the house. James was to kill the boy in the field and the others would take care of the house. They walked their horses to the homestead and were waiting in front of the cabin when the man came out to go to the fields. They had the drop on him and ordered whoever else was in the house to come out. A plump lady of forty-five or so and a nice looking girl of about sixteen came out. Bill stepped down and walked to them acting real friendly like. He stuck out his hand and when the farmer reached to shake it the Mexican shot him straight through the heart. The young girl screamed as the Mexican swung his gun to the left and triggered another shot that struck the woman in the chest. Bill struck the girl hard with his fist, just above the eye, knocking her unconscious.

The boy in the field heard the shots ran toward home and James knocked him down with a bullet in the side. He scrambled to his feet and took off again and James's second shot grazed his skull and he went down to stay. James was sure he had shot him square in the head and didn't bother to check as whether he was dead or not.

The four of them ransacked the house finding bullets and food. Bill threw the still unconscious girl over the back of one of the horses they took from the corral. They were a happy lot, eating biscuits, bacon, and drinking coffee while riding northwest from the homestead. There was a lot of bragging about what each was going to do to the girl when they made camp, except for Robert. He didn't say anything. They made camp later that evening and Robert didn't want to think about what happened after that.

~

Tye reached the infirmary and made his way to where Major Thurston and the Jenkins boy were. The boy was hurting pretty bad. Tye saw immediately it was who he was hoping it wasn't. The boy's eyes opened wide and a slight smile crossed his face as he recognized Tye. Tye placed his hand on the boy's feverish forehead.

"How are you, Todd?"

Todd nodded. "Okay I guess," he said through clenched teeth, trying to smile, and failed.

"What happened?"

"After breakfast this morning I went to the field as usual. Pa would be there shortly. I was waiting on him and putting the harness on old Bill, getting ready to do some plowing, when I heard shots. I jumped up and ran toward the house when I was hit here," he said pointing to his side. "I got up to run again and then things went black. I guess that's when I was hit in the head.

The man must have thought I was dead. I was out for awhile…maybe three hours or so judging by the sun when I came to. I made it to the house and found Ma and Pa lying outside both shot in the heart." Tears welled up in his eyes and his lower lip trembled.

Tye leaned down and spoke softly. "It's okay Todd. Go ahead and let it out." He leaned closer and the boy put his arms around Tye's neck; Tye pulled him to his chest and the boy let all his emotions go. Tye held him till he was spent and lay him back down on the pillow.

"You okay?"

The boy, sniffing nodded his head. Tye spoke again. "What about your sister, Susan?" The boy shook his head.

"I don't know. I could not find her. I'm afraid those men took her." Thurston saw Tye's fist squeezed so tight they were turning white. "You rest up, son. I will find your sister." He leaned down and kissed the boy on the forehead. The boy nodded and shut his eyes as tears rolled from the corners down his cheek. Tye walked outside the infirmary, took a deep breath of the night air and let it out slow, trying to calm down.

"It is apparent that you know the boy, Tye. Were they related to you?"

Tye sighed. "His mother was my mother's youngest sister. I last saw them about six months ago. They have a great place about twenty miles south east of here. It was well kept. They had worked hard and were as happy as anyone I ever saw. Then this…" He looked at Thurston. "I'll be leaving in a few minutes Major. I can be there by daylight and get a handle on what happened and maybe where the bastards went."

"It will take me awhile to get a patrol together, Tye."

"Don't bother, Major. I will handle this one alone."

"ALONE!" Thurston exclaimed. "You heard the boy. These men are vicious."

Tye cut him off. "I'll be fine. Can you get me some supplies together in a few minutes?" He turned and headed toward home. Thurston shook his head in disbelief and then headed to the barracks to get the quartermaster. Tye turned back to him and hollered.

"If you like, get my scout Dan and a small patrol together and have them follow me in the morning. Dan can get an idea of where the homestead is from the boy." He didn't wait for a reply and headed home.

Rebecca was waiting for him on the porch. She could tell by his expression that her fears were correct.

"It was your mother's sister family wasn't it?" she asked, tears running down her cheeks. Tye nodded. "After you left, I remembered you talking about them. I'm so sorry," she said throwing her arms around his neck and kissing him. Tye tasted the salty tears on her lips as he hugged and kissed her back. "I figured you would be leaving, so I have your clothes on the bed."

Tye pulled back and looked into her lovely face. "You know me pretty well don't you."

"You just be careful Tye Watkins and make sure you get back to me...and your baby." Tye kissed her again and went into the bedroom. He pulled off his cotton shirt and pulled on his buckskin shirt. His pants came off next and his faded blue cavalry pants with the yellow stripe were pulled on. He pulled on his knee high Apache leather boots and stuck his Bowie in the sheath that was in the top of his right boot. He strapped on his Navy Colt and grabbed his Henry repeating rifle off the rack. I'm picking up some supplies at the quartermasters before I leave. He kissed his wife again and turned to Buff. "Take care of her old friend."

Buff reached out and shook Tye's hand. "Don't you worry about a thing. You just be careful."

"Always am, Buff," he said heading out the door. He turned his head and looked back at Rebecca. "Love you, Honey." She blew him a kiss and he turned and disappeared in the darkness.

Gary McMillan

Chapter Six

Tye walked the short distance to the stables to saddle up Sandy and then led him to the Quartermaster's to see if Thurston had managed to get his supplies ready. He should have known not to wonder because Thurston ran a tight ship; the officers and men knew better than to be lax in their duties no matter what hour of the day or night. He crossed the bridge over Los Moras Creek and turned east on the Old Mail Road. His old friend Jim that owned the saloon directly across from the bridge was sweeping off the boardwalk in front in front of his establishment gave him a wave that Tye acknowledged. Tye pulled his hat down and kicked Sandy into a gallop.

After a few days in the corral, Sandy was anxious to run and Tye had to keep a tight rein on him to hold him at a steady gallop. The horse was a gift to Tye last year for bringing in the vicious Vasquez brothers. If a man could ever be a friend to a horse and vice versa, these two were. Tye, like most scouts, spent a lot of time alone when in the field; he would sometimes talk to Sandy and he would tell you that Sandy understood every word. Sandy never complained about his off key singing either. Several times in the past, Sandy had saved Tye's hide by letting his master know someone or something was close by twitching his ears or nickering. A horse could see, smell, and hear better than a human, so it was a smart man who paid attention to such things.

It was going to be a long night, so Tye would alternate trotting, walking, and galloping Sandy with a few breaks, so the horse could blow a few minutes. Tye spent most of time when they were resting looking at the vast Texas sky. There was no moon, so the stars were sparkling like diamonds against the black sky. It never ceased to amaze Tye how many stars there were. It was times like this when his thoughts went back to the many nights he and his pa spent under the stars when he was a kid. His pa pointed out constellations and taught him to tell time by the position of certain stars at different times of the year. This is where he told young Tye stories about his years in the mountains with Bridger, Shakespeare, and Stumpy Absher. Sometimes, the stories were about dangerous situations he was in and how he managed to escape them. Tye had remembered these particular stories, and several times in the past had saved his hide by remembering how his pa had escaped similar situations. Even though his pa had been dead several years, remembering those nights under the stars would always bring a lump in his throat. It was as dark as sin, but Tye knew the area so well he rode Sandy in a direct line to the Jenkins homestead. He would find later, much to his consternation; he had ridden within a quarter of a mile from the outlaw's camp. The eastern sky was just turning gray with the coming dawn when he topped the hill above the homestead.

~

Bill, being the first up, had started a small fire and put the coffee on. Within a few minutes the water was boiling; and as always whether it was cowboys, soldiers, or outlaws, eyes popped open as the aroma drifted through the camp on the early morning breeze. The other three men crawled out of their bedrolls, and after putting their hats on, pulled on their boots. It made no difference when you saw a cowboy unless he was asleep, he had his hat on. A cowboy bathing in a creek might be completely naked, but he would probably have his hat on.

Dressed and their guns strapped around their waist, they moseyed over to the fire with their cups. Bill handed each a tin plate with two hot biscuits and bacon he had warmed on the fire. When Running Elk had eaten about half of his first biscuit, he laughed.

"Hell, Bill. This is pretty good. If you weren't so damn ugly I just might marry you." He slapped his leg and he-hawed loudly as did the others...except for Bill.

"You could ask till you are blue in the face and the answer would be no...I wouldn't marry no Mexican and sure as hell no breed." The laughter ceased immediately and it was suddenly so quiet you could hear the water bubbling in the small creek about twenty yards away. The Mexican's eyes flashed fire for a second then he saw Bill smiling. He remembered Bill's killing the girl last night as casual as he would have shot a skunk. He liked the man and he figured he was kidding...at least for now, that was the way he was going to take it. Robert and James relaxed as they saw the smile cross the breeds face.

"Figure we had better get shuck from around here as soon as it's light," Bill said. "I don't want to be around if some one stumbles across that girls body."

"Where you figure?" James asked.

"I hear that Brackettville is pretty lively." Bill replied.

"They have some saloons and where there are saloons there are some ladies," Robert commented, just a little excited of the chance he might get to be with a girl and not feel bad about it.

The breed started laughing and they all looked at him wondering what was so damn funny.

"What's so damn funny?" Bill asked, a little agitated that his idea was somehow funny.

"You wanting to go to Brackettville...that's what," the breed said smiling.

James looked him. "What is funny about that?"

"Any of you ever heard of a scout named of Tye Watkins?" Silence followed his question. "Tye Watkins is Chief of Scouts at Fort Clark, which just happens to be right across the road from Brackettville. He is the most dangerous tracker a man can have on his trail...worse than Apaches. Three or four years ago, when he was with the Rangers, he brought in so many outlaws there was a bounty put on him by some of the outlaws...no one collected. He's over six foot tall, built like a blacksmith and worse than tangling with any two men in a fight whether it is with fist, knives, tomahawks, or guns. He thinks like an Apache, tracks better than most of them, and some say, can be meaner."

"Sounds to me like you are afraid of this here bigger than life man," Bill said laughing.

The breed's eyes flashed again and this time he didn't hold back. He was across the fire in an instant grabbing Bill by the throat with his left hand and pulling his Bowie with his right. Before Bill could even begin to react, the point of the razor sharp Bowie was against his left cheek.

"No one talks to me like that...EVER," he shouted. "I am not afraid of any man, but only a damn fool plays against a stacked deck. You get Tye on your trail; you have the stinking Army on it also." He lifted the heavy Bill to his feet. "You do what you want, but don't ever laugh at me again." He released his hand from the neck of a gasping Bill and shoved him backwards. "Not ever," he repeated.   Bill reached up and massaged his throat.

"You better be looking over your shoulder Breed cause I'm gonna kill you for that one of these days," Bill snarled. The breed laughed and boldly turned his back on Bill and walked away.

~

Tye topped a hill that overlooked the Jenkins homestead. Through the dim early morning light he was surprised to see several soldiers milling about. He was a little confused because he knew no patrols from Clark were in this area and there was no way a patrol left after him and beat him here. He started Sandy down the steep rocky slope dislodging several rocks that made a lot of noise sliding down the hill. Heads of soldiers snapped around at the first sound and they were grabbing their Sharps.

"DON'T SHOOT!" Tye shouted. "I'M COMING IN." He continued on down the slope. Reaching the bottom of the hill he saw an officer riding toward him. At thirty yards, recognition from both men was instantaneous. Both men kicked their horses to close the gap quickly and reined in side by side with the two men reaching to shake hands.

"Lieutenant Rogers." Tye said to his friend from Fort Inge. "What in blazes are you doing out here?

"I'm just following orders."

"What orders?"

"My orders were to pursue these men till we catch them."

"What men?"

"Two brothers, Bill and Robert Baxter, their nephew James, and someone you may know, Miguel Espinosa."

"The Breed?"

"Yes Sir, and he's the worst of the lot as you know."

"I've never seen him but if half of the stories I have heard are true, he's pure poison."

"He's in good company. Bill Baxter is wanted for murder, as is James, the nephew. Bill killed a trooper from Inge in Uvalde the other night. We have been on the trail since night before last."

Tye looked at the troops. "I don't see a scout. Are you doing the tracking?"

Rogers laughed. "You know better than that. I've matured a lot since I last saw you but not that much. Corporal Patton is a fair tracker. He's kept us on the trail. You may remember him. He was one of the men with me in that ambush you pulled us out of several months ago."

"I don't remember the name, but I'll probably remember his face."

"Looks like he is telling the other men who you are," Rogers said nodding toward the group. Tye glanced at the men and quickly looked another direction when he saw they were looking at him. Tye knew he carried a certain mystic, but it always embarrassed him when men made a fuss over his being around.

"What happened here?" Tye asked as they approached the group of men.

"A man and woman are dead over there. Both shot. We haven't found anyone else yet. Patton said he figured it happened early yesterday."

Tye walked over to the two bodies with blankets over them. Kneeling he pulled the blanket from the woman's face. He lowered his head, shut his eyes and silently cursed this land that had so many men in it that have no qualms about killing another human being. He loved this country; but unfortunately, being the hard land it was, it produced hard men. The men and women that settled here were hard, tough folks; but they were good folks, God fearing people for the most part and only wanted to be left alone to live their lives. The problem came when men like the ones who killed this family were just too lazy to work and took what the good people like these had worked for.

"Can you hold your men together for a few minutes Lieutenant?" Tye asked. "I need to look around before any more tracks are added to what was here. Corporal Patton, can you come with me?"

"Yes, Sir," Patton said hurrying to step in behind Tye and following him around the camp. "Did you figure there were four of them," Tye asked.

"I wasn't sure, Sir, but I figured it was three to five."

Tye stopped and turned around and smiled. "If you don't mind Corporal, call me Tye. That 'sir' sort of makes me feel old."

"Yes, Sir...I mean Tye." Tye smiled and slapped him on the shoulder.

The rest of the men were watching Tye walk, stop, backtrack, bend down, stare off in the distance, and then say something to the corporal as they walked a little farther away from camp.

Private Benson just had to ask. "Lieutenant, tell us about Tye. We all understand you know him pretty well and all we have heard is stories."

"I don't know him as well as I would like to. He has led a very interesting life...a dangerous one, but interesting. When I was first assigned to Fort Inge, I was fortunate that Tye and his wife were on the coach headed back to Fort Clark from San Antonio where they had been on their honeymoon. We visited for hours but he never talked about himself much. He talked about the land out here, the people including the Apache, and just what I could expect from the soldiers as far as being an officer fresh from the Point on his first assignment. Most of what I know about him came from his friend, Lieutenant Garrison at Clark."

"Whatever you heard is probably true and probably more unbelievable than the way you heard it. He was born to do what he does. His pa was a well known mountain man; and from the day Tye could walk, he taught him about surviving. Tye learned things like tracking, reading sign, fighting with knives, tomahawks, and even making and handling a bow and arrow. He was taught the art of wrestling and don't ever challenge him to a fight with your fist. He learned how to live off the land. He was born here and is as part of this country as the Apache. He has fought them since he was fourteen; he thinks like one, and can survive out here as well as they can."

"You see how big he is, well, you should see him with his shirt off. He has muscles where you only dream you could have. He has more scars from bullets, knives, and arrows than all the men at Clark put together." Rogers laughed. "He told me one time that the Post Surgeon at Clark told him he would never die because he had no vital organs. I saw him strip his buckskin shirt off to fight a well-known Apache warrior whom he had captured. This warrior called him a coward, a woman, and other vile things in Apache challenging Tye to fight.

"Hell, why didn't he just shoot him," Private Mendez asked?

"Tye has respect from all the Apaches, the outlaws, and especially the troops he scouts for," Rogers answered. "He also has a code of ethics...I'm afraid one that could get him killed one day. He will not shoot a man in the back, even in battle. I heard from a Lieutenant Garrison from Clark that Tye gave the crazy killer Alex Vasquez a chance to fight him man to man after he had captured the famous outlaw because not because of what the man had done to a lot of settlers, but because he just would not shut his mouth as to how he could beat the hell out of Tye if he got the chance. Tye gave him the chance. Tye beat the living hell out the man. He did the same thing with the outlaw Yancey Cates. As far as this Apache was concerned, if the word got around that Tye had refused to fight him, a lot of that respect as a warrior would be lost among the Apache tribes." He watched Tye and Patton disappear around a hill.

"There are a lot of scouts in the army, but none can hold a candle to that man when it comes to tracking, fighting, and keeping his men out of trouble. It's said he is as much Apache as the Apaches. He can smell out trouble before if comes his way. Of all the patrols he has scouted for only one was ambushed and that was because the officer would not listen to him. That officer is a Captain at Fort Clark and is alive due to Tye's getting him and the men out of the trap. He listens now," Rogers added smiling.

"His wife is something else. She is the most beautiful woman I have ever seen...and a real lady." Rogers thought back to that ride in the coach with Tye and Rebecca when he was going to Fort Inge. He would always relish the hours he and Tye talked and Tye telling him about this country and what to expect. He added, "I think what best sums up Tye is that he will do anything to protect a soldier or a settler; even if it meant giving up his life. He pa was killed saving some Rangers who had blundered into an ambush."

"They are coming back." one of the men said and all heads snapped around in the direction the man pointed. They could see Tye and Corporal Patton were in a discussion about things as they came their way.

When Tye came up to the men and Lieutenant Rogers, they all could see he was a little more than upset...he had a look of a man really upset. "There's four of them Lieutenant, like you said . The man and woman over there are Bill and Lisa Jenkins. They have a daughter that the vermin have taken with them. She's about fifteen or so." He held up part of the dress that had been ripped off her and showed it to the men. He then folded it neatly and put it in his saddle bag. "I don't guess I have to explain to any of you what to expect to find when we catch up to these animals. They also shot a young boy. He stumbled into Fort Clark last night just about done in. That's why I came here. If it's okay with you Lieutenant, I'll ride with you and your men till we catch them." He looked every man in the eye one by one and then, in a voice that sent a chill up the men's spines said, "We will catch them and they will pay for this and ever other damn crime they have committed; this I swear to God above. He looked at Rogers for an answer to his question.

"We...I mean I would love to have you go with us and we are as determined as you to catch these men."

Tye mounted Sandy and said in a tone that had a chill to it. "Not in a million years, Lieutenant. Not in a million years. Let's ride" and he turned Sandy and headed out northwest.

"You heard the man...MOUNT UP! Rogers shouted. The men hurried over to their horses and mounted. Rogers said loudly as he raised his arm and dropped it forward, "COLUMN OF TWOS...YO."

He turned in the saddle and said, "Corporal Patton, up here beside me." Patton reined his mount beside the lieutenant. "Tye is pretty upset isn't he?"

Patton spit a wad of the ever present chew. "Yes, Sir, he is. Those folks were relatives of his on his mother's side. He stood in the stirrups and then settled his butt in the hated McClellan saddle. "I sure would not want to be in those boys' boots when he catches up with them. I heard tell that man can be meaner than any Apache when he's riled... and he is definitely that."

Chapter Seven

The sun was well above the hills by the time the outlaw gang broke camp. After much discussion, and arguing, they decided to head west toward Mexico instead of northwest toward Fort Clark. This decision was due to the Breed's insistence of staying away from any chance of Watkins being on their trail. The Breed also convinced them he knew where a couple of homesteads were on the way that they could rob, and how sweet the senoritas were across the Border.

Bill was the only one of the four who wanted to head to Clark as he had previously suggested. He was upset his brother and nephew had sided with the Breed, calling them cowards among other names. He was careful that he didn't include the half-breed in his tirades. He wasn't afraid of the man but he knew in a fight between men who were good with guns, knives, or whatever, even the winner would come out of it hurt pretty bad, so he gave in and agreed to go west. He figured it was that or travel alone toward Clark.

The land was low rolling hills covered in sage, cactus, cedars, and mesquites. Bill couldn't figure why all these people were coming out here because the land appeared to be too rocky for farming and the grass too sparse for running livestock.

"Miguel," he said not wanting to offend him by calling him Breed, "You're from this country aren't you?"

"I was born about fifty miles southwest of here near the Rio Grande. Why?"

"I was just looking at the damn country, that to me ain't fit for nothing, and wondering why all these people were coming and settling here."

The Breed thought for a moment...long enough that Bill didn't think he was going to answer. "These people are different from us. They are men and women with a dream of owning land...a little piece of Texas." Bill interrupted.

"Why own this?" he said sweeping his arm out in front of him. "It ain't worth nothing."

The Breed smiled. "Bill, what do you own?" Before Bill could answer he continued. "You own the same as me; two shirts, two pair of pants, a rifle, a pistol; and don't have a clue as to when you will sleep in a real bed again. Hell, even the horse I'm riding and the food I'm eating is stolen. The people coming out here want what we are too lazy to work for. They want to own some land, even if it's poor land. They want to build a home, raise children, and for the most part to be left alone. The land in some of the valleys is actually good farm land and if there is water, a man can make it."

"They bust their butts and we ride in and take it away. Well, thank you mister farmer." Bill laughed loudly at his own poor joke and then shut up when he realized no one else was laughing. 'I hate riding with men with no sense of humor,' he thought to himself. "To hell with them," he mumbled under his breath.

They rode in single file with the Breed in front and Bill bringing up the rear. They rode in silence with only the clicking of their horses' shoes striking rocks, ringing loudly in the stillness of this parched land. They rode mile after monotonous mile and when they topped a hill there was always another hill, and another with nothing in between but sage and cactus. Bill again wondered why people wanted this God-forsaken-country regardless of the reasons the Breed said earlier.

About mid-afternoon the Breed reined in his mount. "There's a homestead about a half mile farther. We need to wait till almost dark to move in." For once, Bill didn't argue. He wanted nothing more now than to step down off his horse and stretch out on the ground. He had some thinking to do about the situation here. He was still just a little more than put out with his brother and nephew for siding earlier today with the Breed. He was going to do something about it...he just wasn't sure what yet.

~

When the patrol topped the hill, they saw Tye standing beside his horse about a quarter mile ahead of them, apparently waiting for them. The scout stood there watching them come toward him absently scratching Sandy between the ears. He could hear the patrol coming before they topped the hill. He had tried unsuccessfully for the last two years for the army to allow the men to do away with some of the 'required' army issue equipment such as sabers and extra canteens, which were always rattling or clanging. He would like to do away with brass buttons, shiny shoulder bars of the officers, and the crossed swords on the hats. Nothing natural in this country reflected sunlight and the sun shinning off these items was like a beacon for the always watchful Apache. He shook his head and smiled, knowing why the army could never surprise the Apache and never would.

He watched the patrol as they rode up to him. He liked Lieutenant Rogers and thought he was going to make a fine officer. Rogers was on his first patrol several months ago out of Fort Inge, when they were ambushed by a large number of Apaches. The officer in charge was killed immediately; Rogers took over like a veteran officer and led his men to a defendable position in the rocks. He barked orders like he had done this a thousand times and the men responded to this youngster. Tye stumbled onto them by accident and managed to bring the patrol from Clark he was scouting for to bail them out of a tough situation.

As Rogers and the patrol arrived with clanging sabers, squeaking McClellan saddles, and hooves of a dozen horses striking the rocky ground he raised his arm and the patrol came to a halt. The sudden silence was startling and Tye just shook his head. "Heard you coming from a mile away, Lieutenant. I've tried to get the army to change their way of thinking about some of the required gear they always carry, but I might as well been beating my head against a wall. Maybe you can."

Rogers sat in the saddle with both hands on the pommel and leaned forward looking at Tye. "You know the army as well as me and it takes years to change anything," he replied smiling. He noticed a cold campfire. "Was this where they camped?"

"Yes, Sir. They camped here and I rode within a quarter of a mile from them last night on my way to the Jenkins place," Tye answered shaking his head in disgust. "I can't believe I didn't see or smell their fire." Rogers dismounted and handed his reins to the private behind him. Tye nodded toward Mexico. "They are still heading west."

71

"The girl still with them?"

"I don't think so, Lieutenant. The fifth horse's tracks are not as deep as yesterday, indicating less weight being carried. I'm afraid we'll find her around here somewhere. Can you get the men to spread out and take a look?"

Rogers looked at Corporal Patton. "Corporal, spread the men out and sweep the area."

"Yes, Sir," Patton said saluting and turned to the men. "You heard the Lieutenant. Benson, you take Mendez and Brooker and search to the north of camp. Grizzle, Mosley, and James, you three search the south side of camp." The men immediately started their search.

Within a minute Mosley whistled and waved his hat. He was about a hundred yards away. Tye mounted Sandy and galloped with mason and Patton toward the gathering men. When they arrived the men had their backs to the body of the Jenkins girl. Tye walked over carrying a blanket and covered the girl. Tears welled in his eyes as he remembered how pretty and full of life she was the last time he saw her. He knelt down on one knee and placed his hand on her forehead. "Take her to your bosom Lord." He quietly prayed. He gathered himself and looked at the men.

"Gather round me." The men circled him closely. He reached down and pulled the blanket from the girls face. "She was a pretty thing, full of life, and had great expectations of what life held for her. I want each of you to look at her face and remember it. The men that did this are pure animals and I assure you they will be treated accordingly. They will receive no quarter if they refuse to give up…no mercy if they fight." He pointed to the girl and in a demanding tone simply said,

"Remember." The men would not forget. Women were held in high esteem by the vast majority of men in the country and violating one was unthinkable, except for the no-good disgusting type of men they were chasing. Even hardened soldiers like Corporal Patton, who had been around and seen it all, had a lump in his throat looking at the young girl and thinking what she never got to experience in life. It was such a waste and each man was determined to capture or kill the bastards who did this.

They dug a shallow grave and the girl, wrapped in a blanket, was buried and then covered with rocks. A crude wooden cross with her name on it was placed at the head of the grave. Rogers led a short service and then they were on their way, every man more determined than before, to find these four men and bring them to justice…maybe even a real quick justice.

~

Dan August, at the Jenkins homestead, waited on the patrol led by Lieutenant Wright from Fort Clark to arrive. Dan was the best of Tye's scouts and he and the patrol had left Clark before daylight. He had led them to the homestead guided by the directions the boy had written down. While waiting, he had scouted around and found the graves. He was puzzled by the number of horses that had been milling around. He could tell that Tye had headed northwest because not too many horses had a print as big as Sandy's. He was very familiar with Sandy's print since he had followed them from the fort. He could see that maybe seven or eight horses were with Tye who was riding just to the side of the four or five horses tracks that Dan figured were the killers of the Jenkins. Following tracks to the side instead of riding directly behind and over them was a habit of Tye's. If he had a problem with the tracks, he could go back and re-read them, which would be impossible if the patrol rode over them. This was just one of a thousand things the man had taught Dan the last two years. He sat on his horse waiting on the patrol trying to figure out who the men with Tye were. He studied the tracks again and realized they were riding two abreast...

"CALVARY," he said out loud. He knew no patrols from Clark were in the area, so he figured they must be from Inge. He turned and looked over his shoulder when he heard the patrol arriving. He explained the situation to Lieutenant Wright and then suggested they take a break before heading out. The Lieutenant was new to Clark and this was the first time Dan had ridden with him. Dan thought for a newcomer, the Lieutenant handled himself and the men pretty well. The true test of any officer though, would come out when he faced the Apache for the first time. Dan would hold his opinion of the man till then. After a short break they followed Tye.

Gary McMillan

Chapter Eight

The four outlaws lay in the brush no more than two hundred yards from the homestead. The sun would be dropping behind the hills in a few minutes. Breed knew most homesteaders followed the same routine so he figured they would be finishing the evening meal very soon and the man would come out on the porch to smoke. If he had sons, they would probably come also, not to smoke, but discuss the days work and what they had to do the next day.

He had no more than thought this than the door opened and a man of about forty came out with his rifle. He looked around, sat down and lay his rifle beside him, barrel pointed away from the house and the grip handy. Billy Coulter was a careful man...a cautious man and that is why he had survived two Apache raids in the last two years. He lit his pipe but never took his eyes off the hills in front of his home. He had cleared brush for about seventy yards in front and to the south of his home making it hard for anyone to surprise him. He built the house facing east so the hot sun in the summer did not heat the living area and the two bedrooms which were along the front of the house. Made from adobe blocks that were more than a foot thick, the house was cozy in the winter and fairly cool in the summer. The house was built with care, being very sturdy with ceilings ten foot high to allow the heat to rise.

The Breed surveyed the area around the house and cursed under his breath but loud enough for the others to hear. "That old man has a well built house that ain't going to be easy to get to without one or more of us getting shot."

Bill whispered, "There's four of us and one of him. What's the problem?"

The Breed answered him angrily. "If you would take the damn time to look around you would see what I mean. There's an arroyo to the north and I bet you a dollar it runs behind the house. It looks to wide for a horse to jump and I bet you it's deep. That leave the front and south side to approach from and there ain't a stick to hide behind for sixty or more yards in those directions. The old man ain't a damn fool.

"He's a farmer." Bill said. "Probably don't know one end of that rifle from the other."

"Maybe," The Breed said, "But just from looking around I bet he has been here for awhile and if so, he's had more than one encounter with men like us and the Apache and he's still here."

"So, what the hell do you propose we do…just pass them by?" Bill questioned, his impatience with the Breed showing in his voice.

"I have a plan. Let's back down this hill and talk about it." They scooted back down the hill to where their horses were.

"What is this great idea?" Bill asked.

The Breed ignored the tone in Bills voice. He looked at the youngster, James and asked. "Can you pretend?"

James looked at Bill and Robert. "Never thought anything about it…why?"

"Thought maybe with you being so young and innocent looking that you might just get inside that cabin and get the drop on those people. Sure would be better than one or so of us getting shot up if you could."

James looked puzzled. "Where does the pretending come in?"

"I thought that you might go in looking like you had seen better days walking and carrying your saddle on your shoulder with some story about getting robbed by outlaws." He laughed.

James looked at Bill. The older brother thought for a moment the said, "It might just work. Like the man said, it would be better than getting shot if it does." Robert nodded and shrugged his shoulders.

James looked over his shoulder toward where the homestead lay just over the hill they had just come down. "Yeah, I can do it," he said.

"Good," the Breed said. "Let's get your saddle off the horse and get it done before it gets plum dark." They walked over to James's horse and stripped off the saddle. He said he would fire two quick shots for a signal to come in. He walked off carrying his saddle, looking back only once over his shoulder at the three men.

Billy Coulter, ever careful even when relaxing, saw the man as soon as he came around the low hill. "Susie," he said in a low voice. "Shut the windows and get my extra gun and ammunition out and on the table." He hit his pipe on the palm of his hand to get the tobacco out and placed the pipe back in his overalls pocket. The man was over a hundred yards away and appeared to be carrying his saddle or something on his shoulder. His eyes carefully searched the areas to the left and right of the man, seeing nothing. He held the Henry repeater casually but with the barrel pointing in the direction of the man. His finger lightly touched the trigger and his thumb was on the hammer. He walked to the south end of the porch and looked quickly in that direction but saw no movement. He looked back at the approaching man who was now only sixty or so yards out and in the area he had cleared of brush. The man stopped suddenly and dropping the saddle hollered.

"HELLO THE HOUSE." He took a few more steps forward with his hands out so the man on the porch could see he had nothing in his hands.

"WHO ARE YOU AND WHAT DO YOU WANT?" the man on the porch asked loud enough to be understood plainly.

James walked a few more steps with his arms held out. "That's far enough," the man said. "I asked who you who you were and what you want."

"Robert Williams," James answered. "I got jumped by a couple renegade Apaches about three miles back. They shot my horse before I shot them and I couldn't get near to their ponies to catch one. My feet are hurting walking this far and I just want some rest, maybe something to eat. I'll buy a horse if you got one for sale." He said nodding toward the corral where two horses stood watching the men.

" Hadn't got a horse for sale but come in closer so I can get a look at you."

"Is it okay if walk back up and get my saddle?"

The man nodded. "Go ahead but if you make a move to get your rifle from that saddle or that pistol on your hip you will have two holes in you quicker than you can say howdy do." For the first time James saw the other rifle pointing at him from the slot in the wooden shutters that had been shut covering the windows.

"Suspicious damn old man," James muttered under breath as he picked up the saddle. "I'm gonna make him think 'Howdy Do' when I shoot him and whoever has that gun pointed out the window." He started toward the house.

When James was twenty foot from the porch the man said, "Drop you saddle and take off your hat where I can a good look at you." James did as he was told and Billy saw it was a kid who didn't look like he was more than seventeen or eighteen years old. He lowered the rifle and said. "Come on in son. We just finished eating and have some left over that you are welcome to."

"That's mighty nice of you, Sir. I really appreciate it," He said in his best imitation of an innocent young man. He saw the rifle in the window disappear as he stepped on the porch. Walking inside he was actually impressed. The house was neat and clean with a wooden floor instead of packed dirt like most others had. The sparse furniture was all hand made, and made well. The woman who had held the rifle out the window was slim and looked a lot older than she probably was as did the man. He had noticed before that the land out here had a tendency to do that to the people who lived here.

"Sit over here young man," the woman said, pulling a chair from the table. "I'll get you some food and coffee."

"Thank you mam." James said removing his hat. Billy was studying the youngster still not completely convinced he should relax.

"Tell me about the Apaches," he said.

"I don't know if it was Apaches or not. I'm from east of San Antonio and don't know anything about the Indians out here," he said lying. "They were young, maybe about my age, and almost naked. They wore head bands and had knee high buckskin boots."

"Red hand bands?" the man asked.

James though for a moment. "Yes, Sir. Now that you mention it, they were red. Looked like they needed a good washing though. How did you know they were red?"

"Apache for the most part were red hand bands...the sign of a warrior." James nodded as he stuffed a biscuit in his mouth with some real butter on it. He took a swallow of coffee.

"This here biscuit is the best I ever tasted."

The woman smiled. "Maybe it is because you were so hungry."

"Maybe so, ma'am, but all the same it is delicious." He looked around the home again. "Ya'll live here all alone?"

Billy replied. "Our sons, Henry and Robert should be on their way back from Fort Duncan. They left a couple days ago to get some supplies."

"Where is Fort Duncan?"

The man lay the gun down across the table. "Duncan is forty or forty-five miles south and west of here. It's right close to the Rio Grande."

"This venison?" James questioned as he took a bite.

"Antelope," Billy said.

"Right tasty," James said. "I never had any antelope before," he said smiling. The man stood up and turned his back, walking toward the door he had left open. James knew this was his chance so he scooted back from the table and quickly pulled his gun and shot the man in the back. He fired again as the man twisted around to face him. The woman screamed.

Hearing the two shots Bill said, "There's the signal. They had been sitting on their horses waiting so immediately headed toward the home, Robert leading James's mount. "I didn't know if he could pull it off or not," Bill shouted. The Breed looked at him and smiled.

James had grabbed the rifle on the table the man had had and heading toward the rifle the woman had held when the woman screamed again and grabbing a butcher knife, charged him. She had a look of pure hate and when she swung the knife at his belly he stepped back as she swung wildly with the knife and clipped her on the chin with the rifle butt he had picked up. She went down, out cold.

When the three men burst thought the door, pistols out ready, they saw James sitting at the table stuffing biscuits in his mouth. They saw the man on the floor, bleeding and saw the woman crumpled in a corner. Bill walked over to the man and took a close look. He was dead. "The woman dead too?"

"No," James said. "I knocked her out when she came at me with this." He held up the knife.

"Glad to hear she ain't dead. She's not bad looking."

"Ain't ever been no woman bad looking to you, Bill," Robert said.

"What the hell does that mean?" Bill asked angrily.

"'Nothing, Bill. Didn't mean nothing by it."

"There's more food over there," James said pointing to the stove. Robert walked over and put some biscuits and meat on three plates while the Breed got coffee for each.

"They have two sons that should be back here at any time." James said.

"Where are they?" Breed asked.

"They left a couple days ago to get supplies at Fort Duncan."

"Let's get what we need and get out of here," Robert said.

"Not till I have me some fun with this here woman," Bill said.

"Then you will stay here and have your fun by yourself," the Breed said picking up an empty flour sack and filling it with cans of beans, some potatoes, and coffee. James had the two rifles and ammunition and Robert had some of the cooked antelope in another sack. They found some binoculars. "These might come in handy sometime," Robert said handing them to the Breed.

"Don't you figure they have some money?" Bill asked.

I'm sure they do but look at the way this house is built," the Breed said. "You can look till you are blue in the face and you ain't going to find it." He started out the door with Robert and James. "You coming, Bill?"

Bill looked at the woman who had regained consciousness and sat there, with her husband's head in her lap and a dazed look on her face staring out the door mumbling something no one could understand. Bill looked at them and back to the woman. "Oh hell...hold on I'm coming with you." He pulled his gun and shot the woman in the chest.

"That was totally uncalled for, Bill," Robert said. "She was in no mental condition to identify us."

"Maybe not now but she might have come around and could later." Bill spit out then added. "No since taking a chance. You going soft on us, Robert?" Robert didn't answer but he was more than upset at what he thought was another useless killing. He had watched his brother and nephew become more and more calloused as far as taking a human life. He didn't like it one damn bit either.

The four of them mounted, after waiting on James to saddle his horse and rode south to get around the arroyo that ran behind the house. Twenty minutes later they made camp just as full dark set in.

Gary McMillan

Chapter Nine

"What creek is this?" Lieutenant Rogers asked referring to the creek the patrol had camped by.

"Los Moras Creek," Tye answered. "It is the creek that runs through Fort Clark about fifteen miles north of here. It ambles through the country side for miles before empting into the Rio Grande. There is a lot homesteads that have been built over the years along it including the one where I was born. The old homestead is probably about twenty miles from here."

"You still go there?"

"I do whenever I am in the area and not in a hurry. I try to keep the place livable and keep the weeds off my parent's graves."

"You plan to live there again someday?"

"I don't know...maybe. It's a beautiful place," he paused laughing. "At least it is to me. Most people look at this land and wonder why anyone would want to live out here. If I remember correctly, you were that way the first time I met you."

89

Rogers laughed and nodded his head. "You're right about that. My first impressions were not very good but like you told me at that time, I would grow to appreciate it... and I have."

"Coffee is ready, and the biscuits and bacon are hot, Sir," Private James said. Rogers and Tye walked over to where the men were and sat down with them. A lot of officers that Tye knew would not sit with the men and he always like the ones that did. He liked Lieutenant James Rogers.

Corporal Patton sat down next to Tye. "Tye, me and Private Benson are the only ones here, besides Lieutenant Rogers of course, that have met you and talked with you. He pointed to each man and told Tye their names. There was Private Mendez, Private Brooker, Private Grizzle, Private Mosley, and Private James. Tye nodded his head in acknowledgement of each and then looked back at Private Brooker

"Private...you look like you been around awhile. I take it you have been busted in rank a few times." His remarks brought some laughter from all including Brooker.

"Yes, Sir, you are right. Been as high as First Sergeant before but can't get along with officers who go strictly by the book. That's why I like this here young Lieutenant Rogers. He goes by his gut feeling most of the time."

Tye laughed. "If I was a soldier I would probably be busted back lower than a private...probably on permanent latrine duty for the same reason." This bought a round of laughter from everyone.

"We heard your pa was Ben Watkins, the mountain man that some of us had read about in those dime novels when we was youngsters," Private Mosley said.

"Ben was my pa. Like I told the lieutenant a few minutes ago we lived about twenty miles from here. He trapped in those days with a lot of well know men especially Jim Bridger. His best friend though was a man named Shakespeare McDovitt who trapped with Bridger before Ben joined their party. Shakespeare's nick name was Buff and that what he goes by. He lives with my wife and me at Clark and you should see him. He's seventy-one years old and gets around like a man forty years younger. He has been on patrol with me and has even led some himself since he came to Fort Clark. He has impressed every man at the Fort that he's a not a man to mess with. He killed two Apaches in a knife fight about three weeks ago. He's one tough hombre." He took a bite of hot biscuit with bacon and then took a sip of hot coffee from the damnable tin cups.

"We have spent a lot time talking about the Rockies and those days trapping beaver. In fact, that's what we were doing when I heard about the Jenkins family last night."

"How did you become a scout instead of a soldier"? A private asked.

"My pa started teaching me to read sign, track, shoot, and fight as soon as I was old enough to walk. My first nineteen years, until Pa was killed, was spent learning from him. We were with the Texas Mounted Rifles when he was killed while trying to save some men's lives. I tracked down a lot of bandits after that, and I acquired a reputation as a good tracker. The army heard about me; I was offered a job as scout and then promoted to Chief of Scouts. Been doing it ever since."

Rogers spoke up. "If any of you want to be a scout you had better think about it. You are out in front of everyone and an obvious target for bandits and the Apache. Bad things can happen." He looked at Tye. "Take your shirt off Tye and show them what happens to a scout."

"You serious?" Tye asked.

"I've heard some of the men talking about scouts and the fact they make more than a soldier. I think it would be a good lesson to see." Tye reluctantly stood up and looked at Rogers again. James nodded, and Tye pulled his buckskin shirt over his head.

The first thing each man saw was a muscular body like none they had ever seen before. After the shock of seeing the body they begin noticing the scars.

"Pretty aren't they," Rogers said. "And there is a story with every one of them. In fact, you have added some since I last saw you," he said to Tye smiling.

Tye smiled. "Like you said, it's a hazardous job." He proceeded to answer questions about each before pulling his shirt back on.

"All those wounds you have received and I hear you don't think badly of the Apache," Private Grizzle said.

No one said anything waiting for Tye's answer. "I'll answer with the same answer I've given many times to soldiers and civilian that ask me that. No, I don't hate them...I respect them. They have been here a long time and lived free to come and go as they please. This land, as each of you knows, is a hostile place that can kill a careless man; the Apache have adapted to it and have thrived on it. I know of no other people that could have done that with the primitive tools and weapons they have. I know it is hard for you to believe, but they are a people that love to laugh and joke with each other. They are gentle and loving to their children. The Apache are an honorable people. The word lie is not in their vocabulary and stealing from one another is unheard of. They do something else us so called civilized people don't do: they have a great respect for their elders and they make sure they are fed, clothed, and have a shelter over their heads." He paused and took another sip of coffee before continuing.

"Then the Mexicans came, and later the whites, pushing them off the land their forefathers had roamed as free men and slowly taking away their way of life. If I was an Apache, I would fight for my land...my freedom...my way of life with every drop of blood in my body. And another thing before one of you say they are so cruel to prisoners, let me tell you they do nothing to a prisoner that was not done to them first by the Mexicans and then the Texans. Scalping was started by the Mexican when they put bounties on Apache scalps and it made no difference if it was man, woman, or child. They torture a man because of their beliefs; you do not want to meet an enemy in the after life that has all his arms, eyes, weapons, and etc; and the longer it takes a man to die the more strength they get from that man and that's the reason they hate a coward or a man that takes his own life and cheats them of that strength. He stood up and threw what remained of his coffee in the fire.

"The men we are after are worse than any Apache. The Apache kill because he is fighting for his way of life. These men kill people of their own race for the hell of it. They have no morals, no feelings or remorse for what they do. I intend to make them pay for every crime they have committed and make them pay painfully." He turned and walked toward his bedroll and lay down.

Private Benson whispered. "Did you see the expression on his face when he said that last sentence?"

Lieutenant Rogers nodded and answered. "He will catch them and I wouldn't want to be in their boots when he does, and if we are going to help, we had better get some sleep." Each man headed to his bedroll a little more educated about the Apache...and about Tye and his feelings. They also in the last few hours, had seen a man that can be friendly as can be, but also a side that scared them some. Rogers checked the sentry before retiring.

~

Back at Fort Clark, young Todd Jenkins was at Tye's house sitting at the table with Rebecca and Buff. He was still hurting some, but Rebecca had convinced old sawbones to let him out of the hospital and let her take care of him. He looked at Buff.

"You're Tye's pa's friend...the mountain man aren't you?"

Buff nodded. "I was Ben's friend back in the Rockies."

"Tye told me all about you. He's really glad you came to live here. He said he has learned a lot about his pa he didn't know."

"Ben was no bragging man," Buff said. "If he had been, you would have been reading as many stories about him as you do Bridger. He was a man's man and when he was your friend he would die for you. You can't say that about most men who claim friendship."

95

"Did Tye come by to see you and your family often?" Rebecca asked.

"Just when he was in the area. It's probably been six months or so. We saw the soldiers from Fort Inge quite often though. We lived in their patrol area and not Fort Clark's. My sister and I always enjoyed his visits. We kept up with things he was doing from the soldiers from Inge coming by. He has quite a reputation you know." Buff and Rebecca looked at each and smiled.

"So we heard," Buff said and winked at Rebecca. "Reckon it's time to hit the bed. You sleep in my bed Sonny and I'll curl up here on a blanket by the fireplace and pretend I'm back in the mountains sleeping on the ground"

"Mr. Shakespeare I can't ta…." He was cut off by Buff.

"Ain't no arguing about it Sonny. Just go to bed." He walked into the room and came out with a couple blankets spreading them on the floor. "Good night Rebecca and you to Sonny." He turned the lamp down and lay down on the blanket.

Rebecca smiled, knowing Buff wouldn't sleep to well on the floor, but it was nice of him to give up his bed. "Good night Todd," she said, turning to go into her room.

"Nite Ma'am. Nite to you too Buff." Todd said, heading to his room. Buff mumbled something that he didn't understand as he shut the door.

Chapter Ten

The sun was breaking just above the hills when the four outlaws mounted and broke camp. Nothing else had been said about the killings last night. That seemed to be the way things had become as far as Robert was concerned. Killing a man or woman had just become like shooting a rabbit or deer. It was done with no remorse nor even given another thought.

Robert rode trying to think what had happened to cause the family to become this way. The war had been a terrible thing; he and Bill had seen things he would never forget: friends killed or wounded, some with arms or legs blown off, and neither knew how many men they had killed themselves. They had been at the battle of Bull Run where about fifteen hundred of their fellow soldiers were killed or wounded and a like number of Yankees before the bluecoats retreated. That was where their oldest brother and James's father was killed. There had been other battles after that with more friends and comrades killed or severely wounded. Still, others he knew had seen the same thing and apparently resumed a normal life after Lee surrendered.

97

What happened to Bill to make him the way he was…or for that matter, to himself for following along with him? He knew Bill was leading them to a certain death down the road somewhere. He looked back at James and thought he's just a kid, hadn't even lived yet. James could still make something of himself, but he had that wild streak in him just like Bill. He shook his head. We're all going to die hard, and pretty soon he figured.

"Hold up," the Breed said suddenly bringing Robert back from his thoughts. They could hear what sounded like a guitar and men singing some song that appeared to be in Spanish. "Stay here," the Breed said, dismounting and taking the binoculars from his saddle bags. "I'm going up the hill and see who is on the other side."

Reaching the top he lay on his belly looking down on a camp with three men milling around and five sitting by a small fire. One was playing a guitar and the others singing. Being careful of no sudden movements which could attract attention, he raised the binoculars to his eyes. Scanning the camp he smiled. He recognized a couple of the men and knew them to be banditos. He moved back down to the waiting men.

"I know a couple of the men. They can be a bad bunch, so watch what you say." They rode around the hill and came into sight of the camp about a quarter mile away. They saw the instant reaction of the men in camp as they saw them also. In less than ten seconds they were mounted and facing the four approaching men. Fifty yards out the four men reined in and then Breed approached the camp, hands out away from his body. The men in camp were surprised when he hollered.

"Hey Lupe Vasquez, it's me...Miguel Espinosa." The men lowered their guns and came forward. The others did not know the Breed, but they sure as hell knew who he was and they all acted like he was a long lost brother. Bill and the other two hung back a ways waiting. Bill didn't like this situation one bit. He wasn't fond of Mexicans and here he was among a whole damn pack of them. His right hand rested on his thigh close to his gun.

Lupe Vasquez was only twenty three years old and wanting a reputation as a bandit approaching that of his late uncle, Alex Vasquez. Alex and his brother Frank had led a gang that terrorized the area along the Border till he met up with the Army led by that damn scout Watkins that put an end to the gang. Lupe was hoping that the army and Watkins would get on his trail because he was going to kill him for what he did to Alex and Frank.

The Breed introduced Bill, Robert, and James to Lupe and the other men. They all shook hands and Robert watched Bill wipe his hands on his pants after the last handshake. He was surprised his older brother had kept his mouth shut knowing the way he felt about Mexicans. They all sat down around the fire and a bottle was passed around. There was some hard looks when Bill passed the bottle without drinking. The Breed spoke in Spanish and told them Bill had a bad stomach. The lie seemed to pacify them and they went back to drinking and singing.

"What are you doing on this side of the Rio Grande?" Breed asked Lupe.

"Fixing to raise some hell and get that scout Watkins on my trail. I intend to kill him." The Breed laughed.

"What's so damn funny?"

"You wanting Watkins on your tail?"

"I'm going to kill him for killing my uncles, Alex and Frank."

Breed smiled. "Do you know how many men have wanted to kill him, and I'm not including a few hundred Apaches? He is still alive and most of the men wanting him dead found themselves six feet under. He's not someone you want to mess with, and you sure as hell don't want him on your tail because he will never quit until he has you. A lot better men than you and me have found out that the hard way."

"You talk like you are afraid of him."

The Breed's back straightened and his eyes narrowed; he looked Lupe straight in the eye. "I am not afraid of any man, but then again I have lived to be my age because I am not a fool."

Lupe stood up instantly, legs spread and hand close to the butt of his pistol. "Are you calling me a fool?" He demanded.

"A fool is a man that intentionally puts himself in danger. Now think about what I am fixing to say. I'm going to give you some names and if you have heard of them, nod your head. First one is James Mosby; the second is Isaac Estaban; the third is Frank Escobedo; the fourth is Joaquin Mendez and of course Alex and Frank." Lupe nodded his recognition of every name.

"These men were well known banditos," Lupe said.

"They were some of the toughest, meanest men you will ever see and every damn one of them was either captured or killed by Watkins." Breed said.

Lupe relaxed and sat down. Maybe he was a little brash in wanting this man on his trail. He did not know Watkins had brought in or killed all those men...only Alex and Frank. He was aware of each of their reputations and considered the fact he might have been a little hasty in deciding what he had wanted. He was from a small village and Alex was a hero to the villagers. He would raid the Texans and always brought food and clothing back to the village. He knew of some of the things Alex and Frank did were terrible, as did the villagers, but they were all poor and the acts were overlooked for the most part because of what he gave them. He looked at his hands that had killed a man already and wondered if Watkins was on his trail now. He wondered if he would see his next birthday. For the first time, he wished he was still in the village with his friends, working in the fields scratching out a living. Yes he thought, scratching out a living, but expecting a long life...a wife and kids. He talked tough and had a reputation as a fighter but he really didn't want to die...he wanted to live. He made up his mind.

"We will be going back to Mexico tomorrow," he told his men in Spanish.

"Mind if we ride with you?" Breed asked. Lupe nodded his okay.

Lupe stood up. "We will ride in the morning but the rest of this day we will drink, sing, and get drunk" The men yelled their approval, the guitar player started playing, the men sat down and started to sing. More bottles of whiskey appeared and in a few minutes the men were on their way becoming drunk including Bill and James. The Breed and Robert sat off to the side knowing someone needed to stay sober and watch for trouble coming because there was still two hours of daylight left and the camp wasn't exactly hidden from view.

~

Tye and the patrol had been riding steady all day following the outlaws. By the look of the tracks they were no more than three or four hours old and the men seemed to be in no hurry. This bothered Tye some, they should be moving quickly, unless… the men were sure no one had discovered the murdered homesteaders and the girl as of yet and was not following them.

Tye reined in when he saw the jumble of tracks and a small hill in front of Sandy. He dismounted and studied them closer. He saw where one man had dismounted and started up the hill to his right. The others had dismounted but stayed with the horses. He looked at the tracks going up the hill and started to follow them but immediately saw where they came back down and then another set led off around the hill while the one who had gone up stayed with the horses. He decided to follow the second set of tracks that led around the hill.

He stopped abruptly when he saw the homestead. "Damn," he muttered when he saw the horses tracks that mingled with the set of footprints he was following. He knew what he was going to find inside the home. His thoughts were confirmed when he was closer and saw the door open and the stable empty.

He was almost to the door when he heard horses coming. He looked over his shoulder and saw two riders coming. At the same time, Rogers and the patrol appeared around the hill. The two riders pulled up looking at the patrol, then at Tye and back to the patrol. They trotted their mounts toward Rogers and the patrol.

Rogers waited until they were close and he turned in the saddle.

"Hold the men here, Corporal." He turned back in the saddle and nudged his horse in the flanks and trotted to meet the two riders. He realized before they met they were both young, probably in their teens. When they met he immediately asked,

"Who are you?"

The older of the two boys spoke up. "This here is my little brother Robert Coulter and I'm Henry Coulter."

"Where are you going?"

"There," he said pointing to the homestead. "We live there with our ma and pa. Why the questions and what are ya'll doing here of you don't mind me asking and who is that by our cabin?"

"We are trailing four men...outlaws and their trail led here." He nodded toward the home. "That man over there is our scout, Tye Watkins."

"Really...we've heard about him. You say their trail led here?" He looked at he home and realized the door was open and no sign of their parents. "OH MY GOD" he hollered and jammed his heels into his mounts flanks and ran hard to the house. He was dismounting even before his horse had come to a halt. He ran into the house with his little brother and Tye on his heels. Both boys stopped in their tracks when they saw their parents. Tye hurried over to make sure they were dead, but he knew that before he touched them. He knew they would be dead when he saw the open door and he was mad...killing mad at this waste of human life. He let the air out of his lungs, looked up at the boys, and shook his head.

The younger boy, Robert, looked at his older brother. "What...how...how could this happen?" He then fell to his knees and took his mother in his arms weeping. Henry stood like a statue, tears running down his face, not know what to do. Rogers came in and sizing up the situation immediately, bent down and gently grabbed the young boy's shoulders and lifted him to his feet. He put his arms around the youngster's shoulders.

"Let's go outside for a minute." Tye stood up and took Henry by the shoulder and led him outside also saying, "We will take care of your ma and pa son. You go care for your brother." Henry put his arm around Roberts shoulder and together they walked to the far end of the porch and sat down.

"What happened here?" Rogers asked while looking at the grieving boys.

"From the sign, it looks like one of the men came in alone and somehow got into the house and killed the man. The woman appeared to be shot a little later. I'll tell you something Lieutenant; these animals are as bad as they come. From what I can tell there was absolutely no reason to kill that woman other than just pure damn meanness."

Rogers took his hat off and his kerchief. He wiped his face and the band inside his hat with it before putting his hat back on his head then retied the kerchief back around his neck. He had seen a lot since coming to this land a year or so ago but he still was shocked at how much violence was here. "Makes you wonder why God made men like that," he commented.

"I don't think God had anything to do with it Lieutenant. Some men are just naturally aggressive and vicious and if you check, a lot of the time their old man was the same way. Some men are that way because of things that happen to them and it turns them against mankind like what just happened here," he said looking at the boys and hoping their up bringing would prevent them from going the way these men were. "I think that most of them are just men too lazy to work; they turn to stealing, which sooner or later leads to killing, and after a few killings they eventually just don't care anymore."

"You're probably right." Rogers turned to the men. "Corporal Patton."

Patton, standing by his horse came forward quickly. "Yes Sir."

"Have the men dig two graves wherever the boys over there want them, and then wrap the man and woman in a blanket. We will have a short service in twenty minutes."

"Right away, Lieutenant." Patton turned back to the men and began barking names and orders for each.

Tye walked over to the boys and sat down. "You two okay?" Neither boy looked up but nodded their heads. "I lost my pa when I was nineteen and my ma a year later. I know you're wondering why this happened. I know in your mind is anger and I know you want some sort of revenge. I figure you are a little confused, worried, and nervous about what's going to happen now."

Henry looked up at Tye. "What did you do when your pa was killed?"

Tye thought for a moment before answering. "I didn't mention that my pa died in my arms telling me he loved me and for me to take care of ma. I grieved like you are doing and then went on about living. That's what you two have to do. Look at this place. Your ma and pa put everything into building this place and they built it well. I'm sure they wanted both of you to continue keeping it that way."

"What about the men that did this," the younger Robert asked, anger replacing grief in his voice?

"I am going to catch them and I promise you they will pay dearly for your parent's lives and the others they have killed."

"Can we come with you," he asked?

"I don't think that would be a good idea, son. What I think you two need to do is rest up today, and in the morning, get back to work taking care of this place. Work is the best medicine; I promise you. When we catch the vermin that did this I will make sure they are brought back through here so you can get a look at them. If they are still alive, I promise you they will hang at Fort Clark and you can have a front row seat."

The men had the graves dug and the bodies were wrapped and lowered with ropes into them. Rogers led a short service and each soldier came by and either shook each boys hand or patted them on the back and had a word or two for each. After the service Tye asked them if they knew where Fort Clark was. They had an idea but had never been there.

"If you need anything or just want to be around some folks go east about three miles and you will come to a creek. That is Los Moras Creek and if you follow it north it will take you to the fort. Look up Major Thurston and tell him what has happened. If you are hungry, ask the major where I live and tell my wife to fix you something. She's a good cook."

"And the prettiest girl in Texas," Rogers said smiling.

Chapter Eleven

Darkness fell on the outlaw's camp. Robert and the Breed were the only men that were awake. Robert could not believe how much liquor the men had consumed. He looked at them as they lay in various positions: four actually made it to their bedrolls, two were asleep sitting upright, chins resting on their chest and both were in danger of falling to one side or the other, and three lay on the bare ground. Most of them were snoring loudly. Bill and James along with one of the Mexicans were asleep leaning up against a pile of large boulders. The rocks looked out of place with all the small rocks in the area. They looked like they had been placed there by people long ago. In spite of himself, he had to smile at the sight of the men passed out in all the different positions.

Breed wasn't so glad to see the men like that. There were patrols in the area as well as scattered renegade Apaches bands. There would be no chance of these men defending themselves if either showed up.

"Looks like it's me and you Robert," he said. You want the first watch or the second?"

"I'm bushed," Robert answered. "I had rather take the second."

"Fine, "the Breed said. "I'll wake you in four hours." Robert found a place for his bedroll, laid down and was soon asleep.

Breed looked at the men and shook his head. A sorrier bunch of so called bad men I've have never seen. Bill and James bad are as they come, but the rest...he spit on the ground. He looked at Robert and figured he was the only one he could trust to do what he said. He knew he was not like his brother as far as just plain mean, but he was one to stand with you when things got tough.

He thought back to his own life of killing and wondered if things would have been different if his parents had not been murdered. He was only nine at the time and witnessed his parents killed. He was spared only because he had been in the barn when the riders came. They called his father an Indian lover and his mother some terrible names. When they shot his parents, he scrambled under some saddles and harnesses that were in the corner of the barn. The men came into the barn, but in the dim light they could not see him. They took a kerosene lamp from the house and threw it against the porch. The lamp burst into flames engulfing the front of his home.

He recognized three of the four men. It took him three years working for a family that had been his mother's and father's friend to earn enough money to buy an old single shot Sharps and thirty rounds of ammunition. The man he lived with taught him to shoot to where he could at least hit in the vicinity of what he was aiming at. A year later, at thirteen, he killed the first of the men that had murdered his parents. The man had a questionable character so no one paid much mind to his killing. Six months later, he killed the other two that were working on a ranch a few miles away.

Everyone figured out who did the killings because in the past, the youngster had let it be known he would do it, but no one paid him no mind, not even the men he ended up killing. He headed to the hills when a warrant for his arrest was issued, and he had been robbing and killing ever since. At first, it was just to have food to survive, but then the life he was leading became easy. He had been on the move ever since, always a step ahead of the Federales in Mexico and the Rangers in Texas. He smiled and shook his head thinking how his life was; always on the move, always looking over his shoulder, never trusting anyone, certainly having no friends, and never experiencing the love of a woman or raising children. He thought of other kids his age when he attended school and the constant name calling because of who he was. He was like a leper, left alone and to be shunned at all cost. What a waste he thought as he stared into the darkness surrounding the camp. A lonely coyote talking to the moon was the only sound he heard. "That's appropriate," he mumbled and settled back against the rock to watch and listen.

~

Tye was leading the patrol of Inge soldiers out of camp well before daylight. The trail of the men headed west and was not varying except to go around a hill or arroyo every once in a while. He figured they would continue doing this, so to close the gap between the soldiers and the outlaws, he decided to take a chance and headed west into the darkness. He was not out front as usual but rode beside Rogers. No one spoke and the only sound was the hoofbeat of the horses and an occasional squeak of a saddle.

As soon as it was light enough to see he told Rogers to hold up the patrol. He scanned the ground for tracks but saw none. He rode left for two hundred yards and saw nothing. Back tracking to the patrol, he rode the opposite way and had ridden no more than fifty yards, and to his relief, found the trail. At the same time he found the tracks, something else got his attention...smoke. He sniffed the air and there was a trace of smoke. He signaled for Rogers to stay where he was.

Dismounting, he tied Sandy to a mesquite and moved west on foot, into the slight breeze. Taking his time he scanned the area in front very carefully. The scent was stronger now and he knew it was a campfire. He also knew it was close. There was a low hill forty yards in front and he started toward it when he heard a horse snort from somewhere in front of him. He dropped behind a thick.sage searching the area carefully. On his hands and knees he started up the slight rise and reaching the top dropped to his belly behind a thick cedar. Parting the thick foliage with his hands, he peered through and saw the camp no more than fifty yards away. He was expecting four men, but there must have been a dozen or so. He looked at the horses picketed on the other side of camp. A quick count totaled fourteen, some of which could be pack horses.

A dozen armed bandits painted a whole new picture on the situation. He figured they could flank the camp and probably succeed in killing or capturing the men but at quite a loss of soldiers in the process. Then again, was the men he was after with this bunch?

The camp was not stirring yet which surprised him. He moved back down the incline to where Sandy waited. He untied the reins and held his hand over the horses' nostrils to keep him from snorting, and led him back to where Rogers was waiting after signaling Rogers to wait where he was.

113

"What did you find, Tye?"

"There's a camp just over that rise yonder," Tye answered nodding his head in the direction of the hill. There's about a dozen men there."

"A dozen," Rogers repeated. "How could that be?"

"I don't know if the men we are after are there. I hate to go charging in shooting and find out they weren't." Rogers nodded.

"Is there anyone in your troops that would recognize any of the men," Tye asked?

Rogers turned in the saddle. "Private Mosley." A man reined in beside the Lieutenant.

"Yes Sir."

"Mosley, were you not in town the night of the killing?"

"Yes Sir. I was there and so was Grizzle."

"Would you recognize any of the men?"

Mosley thought for a moment. "I would recognize the Breed. I've seen him more than once and Grizzle has played cards with him."

"Good enough. I want you to get Private Grizzle and go with Tye. There's a camp over that rise yonder," he said pointing. "See if the Breed is there." Mosley saluted, left and returned in a moment with Private Grizzle.

"Let's go," Tye said quietly. They left their mounts and walked the quarter mile to the base of the small hill and then on all fours, quietly crawled up to the top. The three men watched the camp as men started to stir. It looked liked they had been wrong because it was all Mexicans. They all saw the blonde hair of a white man at the same time as he stood up. Tye's arm was gripped by Grizzle and the soldier nodded to the right of camp. Coming out of the brush was a tall slender man who looked Mexican.

"That's the Breed," Grizzle whispered.

"That's him alright," Mosley whispered from the other side of Tye. Tye nodded and began backing down the slope with the two soldiers following. After scooting backwards twenty feet they stood up and hurried down the slope and back to the patrol.

Rogers walked swiftly to meet them. "Was it them?"

"It's them alright, Lieutenant," Tye answered. "The problem is that we are not only out numbered, but you can bet your last dollar they have these," he said holding up his Henry repeater. "We will be out gunned too."

"What do you think we need to do?"

"We can do what the Apache does...trap them in a place of our choosing. We can..." The unmistakable sound of cavalry interrupted him.

"Soldiers coming, Sir," one of the troopers said.

"I'll be damned," Tye said looking at the approaching patrol.

"Are they from Clark," Rogers asked?

"Yes sir. That's one of my scouts Dan August leading them. I'd recognize the way he sits a horse from a mile away." Tye said smiling, watching as his old friend approached them. Tye walked away from the men toward Dan and the approaching soldiers.

Dan wore a smile on his face as big as Texas. "You are a hard man to catch up with," he said still smiling.

"I thought maybe you would show up sometime and you picked at a good time."

"What's going on?" he asked as Lieutenant Wright and the patrol from Clark rode up. Tye nodded to the lieutenant.

"We have a situation here Lieutenant and your arriving just solved a big problem."

Wright dismounted. "What do we have?"

"Over that rise," Tye said pointing with his Henry, "are a dozen hard cases including the men we are after who killed the Jenkins family. Excuse me," he said realizing he had made no introductions. "Dan...Lieutenant Wright, this is Lieutenant James Rogers from Fort Inge. They were at the Jenkins place when I arrived and have been chasing the four men I said were with that group over the hill. One of the four killed a soldier from Inge in Uvalde." After the introductions and handshakes, Tye continued.

"Like I said, there are a dozen of them and they probably have repeating rifles so we need a plan and have to carry that plan out perfectly to keep casualties to a minimum."

"Lieutenant Wright spoke first. "What do you have in mind?

They all dropped on one knee as Tye, picking up a small stick, began making "x's" on the ground. "Lieutenant Rogers, you have your men here," he said marking an "x" in the dirt. Spread them out along the base of the hill I pointed out a few minutes ago. I will take Wright and the men from Clark south around the camp and charge from the opposite side. They probably won't stand and fight against cavalry patrol so be ready when they run and head away from us over that hill and straight into your guns. Have your men scattered in a rough line at the base of the hill. Have them fire their Sharps and then use their revolvers. They won't have time to reload the Sharps." He cursed under his breath again for maybe the hundredth time over the last two years when he thought of all the times the army was outgunned because of their stubbornness and reluctance to change from the old single shot Sharps. After making sure the plan was understood by all, Tye, Dan and the patrol headed south, to get around the outlaws camp.

Rogers had two men take the horses into an arroyo and picket them. When the men returned he placed then as Tye instructed. Each man was behind a boulder or a thick sage bush

117

and would not be seen until they rose up to fire. Rogers also instructed them not to fire until he gave the order. He was in the middle with the men on each side scattered for about fifty yards along the base of the hill. The men, for the most part, were young and inexperienced. Rogers had done the right thing by placing Corporal Patton and Private Benson, veterans who could be counted on in a pinch, on the opposite ends of the defensive line. They, along with Rogers being in the middle, would hold things together. It had only been five minutes since Tye had left, but to the youngsters it seemed a lot longer. They would wait…they were ready.

.

Chapter Twelve

Twenty minutes passed before Tye and the patrol was on the opposite side of the outlaw's camp. Tye had discussed with the two officers the possibility of the men the four were with not being outlaws. The conclusion was if they ran at the sight of the approaching patrol, chances were they were bandits on this side of the Border and up to no good. If they did not run then there was the chance the four could be taken without much bloodshed... maybe if they were lucky...none.

When the patrol was in position, Lieutenant Wright had them advance toward the camp. They shifted from the standard position of a patrol of riding two abreast into a skirmish line with Tye and himself in the middle and slightly in front. Strict orders were given they would be no firing until he gave the order.

The outlaw's were preparing to break camp. The horses were saddled and two or three men were mounted when the soldiers appeared, suddenly coming over the crest of the hill to

119

the west of them. A shout went up from one of the men and all heads turned quickly toward the patrol who was no more than a hundred yards away.

The Breed stared at the big man in the buckskin shirt in front of the shoulders. He turned to Lupe.

"Well, you wanted to meet Watkins…there he is big as life and coming to get you." He laughed as he mounted his horse. "Go get him, partner," he said with a sneer. Lupe looked at the man the Breed had pointed out and a cold chill went up his spine and the thought of a rope around his neck entered his mind.

Lupe quickly mounted and shouted to his men   "LET'S RIDE." He and his men along with the four white men headed up the slope away from the approaching soldiers.

"CHARGE," shouted Lieutenant Wright and kicked his mount into a dead run. "FIRE AT WILL." Tye had already jumped Sandy out in front and was ten yards ahead of the patrol. Gun's fired from all around him at the fleeing men, but firing from a running horse made hitting anything pure luck. None of the outlaws fell from their mounts as they disappeared over the crest of the hill.

The distinct boom of Sharps rifles sounded as the patrol from Inge opened up. Four outlaws somersaulted of the back of their mounts as heavy lead slugs tore into them. Robert Baxter was the lucky one as he was hit in the shoulder and not the chest as the others. As he fell from his mount, the outlaws reacted and pulling their side arms fired back at the soldiers. Two lucky shots struck two of the soldiers and then young James Baxter and two more of the Mexicans were knocked from their horses. The remaining outlaws made it through the soldiers riding fast, lying low in the saddle.

Tye and the men with him, were through the line of defense and on the outlaws horses tails, no more than fifty yards behind. Tye, holding Sandy's reins between his teeth, raised his Henry to his shoulder. He took careful aim at the man in the rear and squeezed the trigger. The Henry bucked against his shoulder and the man arched his back and then slid sideways off his horse and hit the ground hard. Tye lost sight of the others when they went around a large mound of huge boulders. He slowed down as the soldiers caught up with him. He reined Sandy to a halt and for a moment the only sound was the heavy breathing of the horses.

"What did you stop for," Wright asked? "We were right behind them. WE HAD THEM...WHY DID YOU STOP? He voice rising in anger.

"The Breed is smart and if he is still with them and out of our sight for a few seconds just might give him the idea to stop, turn around and unload some lead as we rounded those boulders. That's exactly what I would do if I was him."

"YOU ARE NOT HIM," the lieutenant spat. He turned to his men who had heard what was said between the men. "LET'S GO," he ordered and jumped his horse away from Tye toward the boulders. The men took a quick look at Tye and then obeyed orders kicking their mounts and following the lieutenant.

"NO LIEUTENANT...NO," Tye screamed. "Damn," he said to himself as he kicked Sandy and followed the men. As the Lieutenant and the men rounded the boulders they met a rain of bullets from the outlaws repeating rifles. Wright and three men hit the ground. The rest of the men stopped, scrambling into the shelter of the boulders, leaving the men where they fell.

Tye pulled up before he rounded the boulders and reined Sandy to the right. The boulders stretched for over a hundred yards and he intended to get around them and hit the men from the flank or maybe he would be lucky and be behind them. "Stay here with them Dan. Try and keep them alive till I get back." Going around the boulders on this side is what he wanted the lieutenant to do but the man didn't wait long enough for him to explain things.

"Don't move Lieutenant," Corporal Patton said in low voice from the boulders. He had heard a moan from Wright and knew he was alive. "If they know you are still alive they will shoot you again." Patton heard no more sounds from the lieutenant so he was either dead or had heard what he had said. The lieutenant was a brash young officer but Patton liked him and hoped he was alive. He knew the lieutenant should have listened to Tye as did the rest of the men, but he wasn't the first officer not to do that. Some had lived to become good officers and others had died because they paid their scouts no mind. He ducked behind the boulders like the others as several rounds of bullets began striking the boulders and ricocheting dangerously in all directions plus rock fragments and where they hit flesh, left cuts.

Tye, figured out the location of the men by the sounds of the second round of fire, and knew he was going to be a little behind the outlaws. He dismounted and crawled to a spot behind a boulder that had some small cactus growing out of it. Plants like the cactus never ceased to amaze him at their ability to grow in this dry country even as these did, growing out of cracks in rocks. Taking off his hat he peered over the boulder and through the cactus. He saw two white men and two Mexicans about fifty yards away. It would be like shooting fish in a barrel with the Henry…for most men, but not Tye. He would never shoot a man he didn't give a chance to give himself up first and sure would not shoot a man in the back.

He sighted down the barrel at the closest man and hollered, "DROP YOUR GUNS."

All four men turned at the same time and opened fire not knowing for sure where the voice was coming from. Tye opened up with the Henry as fast as he could pull the trigger. When the smoke cleared, two men lay on the ground and the sound of running horses reached his ear. He walked to the men and with the toe of his moccasin boot, rolled each over while holding the Henry with the barrel pointed at their heads and his finger on the trigger in case they were not dead. They were both Mexicans and dead as a old piece of drift wood. He hurried back to Sandy, mounted, and rode to where the patrol had taken cover in the boulders.

He found Dan and the others helping the men who were down. Wright was alive but hit hard high in the chest on the right side. Tye thought the wound was high enough to miss the lungs but knew the lieutenant was in some misery. Two of the men were dead and the other was hit in the shoulder.

Tye knelt down by the lieutenant and Wright looked up at him. "That was damn stupid of me, Tye. I should have listened to you."

Tye smiled. "You'll live to learn from it, Lieutenant. The bullet went clean though and I think it missed your lungs and bones. You'll be up and around in a couple weeks."

"Two men are dead because of my stubbornness."

"That's true…two men are dead because you didn't listen. You made a mistake and men died. That's what being in command is all about…making decisions. Some of the ones we make turn out wrong and the consequences sometimes are bad, but if we can learn from that mistake, then maybe lives will be saved later if that situation comes up again." Tye stood up and looked down at the officer and smiled. "Besides, if you smart-ass officers never made a mistake and knew everything about everything, men like me and old Dan here would be out of work." All the men laughed and even Wright smiled…and then grimaced as a fresh wave of pain hit him.

"You men wrap those two soldiers in blankets and make the lieutenant and the corporal as comfortable as possible. I'm going to check on Lieutenant Rogers and his men so you wait here." Mounting Sandy he headed back to the hill.

Rogers had his men assembled around the three men that were lying on the ground when Tye rode up.

"How much damage, Lieutenant?"

"Two dead, one wounded of my men and five dead and three wounded of the outlaws. Two of the wounded are white men. One of them, the younger of the two is unconscious but the other one is sitting over there."

125

Tye walked over and looked at the man who was holding his left hand on his right shoulder. "What's your name?" Tye asked. The man just stared at the ground.

"He would not tell us anything either," Lieutenant Rogers stated.

Tye tuned and as he walked away said, "Oh, he will tell me what I want to know before I get through with him. I knocked a man off his horse over there," he nodded in the direction he was walking. "I'll be back in a minute." He found the man where he fell, a hole in his chest where the bullet exited. Rogers had sent two troopers with him and they picked the man up and carried him back to the others.

"Lieutenant," the white man said to Rogers who turned to the man. "What did that man mean when he said I would talk?"

"That man is Tye Watkins. He's Chief of Scouts at Fort Clark and that family you and your friends killed was relatives of his and he is a little more than upset."

"You didn't answer my question."

"Watkins is more Apache than the Apache. Even they are afraid of him. I've seen him when he's mad and I would not want to be the object of his anger. I don't really know what he means to do to get you to talk, but if I was you I would not want to find out."

"Tye's coming in with another outlaw," a trooper said. They turned and saw Tye coming with the troopers who were carrying a body. When the men arrived they lay the body with the others and Tye walked over to the Lieutenant.

"Two got away and I need to get after them so I don't have time for a lot of unanswered questions," he said looking at Robert. "All the dead were Mexican. I want to know who I am going to be after," he said walking over to Robert. Robert didn't say anything, just stared at the ground. The reached down and grabbed his collar with his left hand and jerked him to his feet and hit him in the belly with a right that had all he could muster behind it. Robert doubled over and fell on his side holding his stomach. Tye rolled him on his back. "Give me names," he demanded. Robert just groaned some so Tye stepped on the hole in his shoulder and ground the sole of his moccasin into it. Robert screamed.

"NAMES," Tye repeated and shifted more weight to the man's wounded shoulder.

"BILL BAXTER AND A MAN CALLED BREED, "Robert screamed.

Tye took his foot off the wound. "And you are?"

"Robert Baxter."

"Bill's Brother?" Robert nodded.

"And the kid over there?"

127

"Our nephew, James Baxter."

"Neither of you will see another birthday unless it's in the next few days," Tye said angrily. "You two are gonna hang and I'm damn sure going to be on the front row along with that couple's young boy that ya'll shot but didn't kill. Hell fire ain't good enough for the likes of you." Robert didn't say anything, just hung his head and wondered again how he got to this place, this terrible ending of his life. Right now he hated that damn high tempered brother of his. It's all his fault... damn him.

"Truss him and that other one up tight," Tye said to Rogers. "Make sure they don't escape. Since you were after them first, take them back to Inge. Let me know when the hanging is." He mounted Sandy. "I'm going to take a couple of men and bring in the ones that got away."

"Be careful Tye," Rogers said. "And thanks again." Tye tipped his hat in acknowledgement and left in a hurry. Rogers watched him ride away. Twice now since he had been at Inge, Tye had helped him. He knew he probably would not have caught up with those men before they got to Mexico without him and he knew for sure he wouldn't even be alive if Tye had not pulled him and his men out of the trap by the Apaches a few months ago.

Arriving to where he had left Wright and the troops from Clark, Tye dismounted, and hurried over to where the lieutenant lay. "How are you doing, Lieutenant?" Tye immediately knew that was a dumb question. Just the expression on the lieutenant's face told him that. "Two men got away, Lieutenant and they are the worst of the lot. Bill Baxter is wanted for murder at Fort Inge, the two families we found and the other...he's worse. The second man is the man known as the Breed and he is pure poison. He kills without a second thought and he's half Apache, which makes it double tough. He knows all the tricks of hiding his tracks, ambush, and every other little trick the Apache knows."

"I take it you are going after them?" Lieutenant Wright said.

"Right away. I stopped here to see if I could get a couple men from you."

The lieutenant grimaced as he raised himself up on one elbow. "Take Dan of course," and then he looked at the men. Privates, O'Riley, Washington, and Langley saddle up and go with Tye. "How far are we from Clark," he asked Tye?

"A half day or so," Tye answered. "Just head north to the Old Mail Road and turn east.

"Private Jameson," he said, laying back down flat on his back breathing heavily from the exertion of the last minute or so.

"Yes, Sir," Jameson said stepping forward.

Wright looked up at him. "Gather up all the ammunition, jerky, coffee, and any other supplies Tye will need.

"Yes Sir."

Dan came in with the material to make a travois for the lieutenant. While Dan made the travois Tye looked over the horses and selected three for the privates to ride. He didn't care about horses that were fast but rather horses that looked like had some bottom to them... staying power. He knew stamina was more important in this case than speed. He knew Dan's horse and of course Sandy was as good as they come. He also took the mounts of the dead soldiers from both Clark and Inge so they all could change horses every so often.

Dan had the travois ready in five minutes and had the lieutenant lying on it as comfortable as possible under the circumstances. When everything was ready, Tye and the men headed west and the lieutenant and three men headed north with the wounded and the bodies of the dead soldiers. Tye was afraid this was going to be a dangerous, bloody chase.

Chapter Thirteen

Breed, Bill and Lupe Vasquez slowed their horses to a walk. Breed figured it would take a while for the soldiers to sort out things before heading out after them. He knew they would take care of the dead and wounded first which as far as he was concerned was stupid…but it would help him get farther away.

"We are going to have to go straight to Mexico and not slow down to eat or sleep. I figure we can be there mid-day tomorrow. Crossing the Rio Grande is the only thing that will stop the army now but it may not stop Watkins." He looked at Lupe. "You wanted the scout, well by God, now you will have him. He'll be on our trail like a damn bloodhound and we are going to have hell losing him."

"Who the hell is this man that has the whole damn frontier shaking in their boots?" Bill asked. "You talk like he is some sort of extraordinary man capable of doing miraculous things. Well, you can shake in your boots at the thought of this man but I bet if you shot him in the ass he would bleed just like you and

131

me." He spit a wad of tobacco juice at a rock. "Yep...he's just a man...nothing else."

"What you say is true," Breed said. "He will bleed like any normal man but a hundred or more outlaws have thought the same thing the last few years...men tougher than you and me and they are all dead... and now he is chasing us." He pulled his horse up and looked at Bill. "Lupe there wanted to meet this man and kill him. You want to see if he bleeds so why don't both of you stay here and see if you can accomplish what so many others couldn't...kill him. Me, I'm riding to Mexico." He kicked his mount and galloped off leaving the two. Bill looked at their back trail as did Lupe. They looked at each other and without saying a word; both kicked their horses and galloped after Breed.

~

Tye found his way back where the men had stopped to ambush the soldiers as they rounded the rocks. He found where the outlaws had left their horses with a man while they attempted the ambush. When he mounted and begin following their tracks, there were three sets instead of the two he expected. He knew before this was going to be a dangerous chase but now with three men, it became more so.

"You men get set for the hardest ride you have ever had. Those men are headed to Mexico and they have almost an hour head start. They know we are going to be hot on their trail so they are not going to waste time stopping to make coffee or for any other reason.   We can catch them with a little luck and a hard ride, so stay with me".

Not many men on the frontier were better horseman than Tye. He knew just how far he could push a horse without ruining him. Tye headed west and the men followed him, their horses at a comfortable gallop. Tye, staying just left of the outlaw's tracks had no problem following the tracks of running horses. Dan rode to his left and watched for places a man with a rifle could hold up and offer a surprise while Tye kept his eyes on the tracks.

The terrain in this part of the country was fairly flat with only gently rolling hills. It would change as they got closer to the Border but for now there were not many places a man could hide and ambush someone. The land was sparsely covered in sage, cactus, and occasional clumps of mesquite breaking up the skyline of a land that seem to go on forever.

Twenty minutes later and after a few miles under their hooves, Tye pulled his second horse beside Sandy and jumped from Sandy into the saddle of his second mount. Each of the

133

men followed his lead. Five minutes later he pulled up and studied the tracks.

"I was wondering when they were going to start walking their mounts," Tye said to Dan. "Much farther and the horses would flounder leaving them, a foot." The tracks of walking horses were not going to be as easy to follow. Tye dismounted and studied the tracks closely. No one said a word; the only sound being the heavy breathing and snorting of the horses. Tye stood up, looking the direction the outlaws were headed. They had closed the gap more than he had thought. They were close...close enough to be real careful.

"We may need to slow down some Tye. Looking at those tracks we are only minutes behind them," Dan said, leaning down from his horse and studying the tracks. "We might just walk into a beehive if we aren't careful." Tye nodded and mounted his horse. The other men nudged their mounts to where the two scouts were.

"We are just a few minutes behind them so we need to have a plan if we come on them suddenly," Tye said. "If they make a run for it which I figure they will, I want each of you to jump back on your original horse and release the reins of the other mount and let him loose. Our mounts should be a lot fresher than their so I think maybe we can run them down and force them to make a stand."

"How far are we from the Border?" Private O'Riley asked.

Tye thought for a moment before answering. "About fifteen miles... give or take a mile or so either way. In three or four miles the terrain will begin to change and there will be more places they can hole up and try to pick us off. If that happens, at the first shot everyone hit the ground and find a hole to crawl in. What happens next will depend on what they do. I've seen men stop and fire a couple shots to simply make the men chasing them hole up for awhile while they put some distance between the two parties. Then again, they may hole up and make a fight of it. A lot will depend on the condition of their horses. Breed knows this country, so I'm sure he knows how far it is to the Rio Grande and the Border and if his horse will make it or not. He's not above sacrificing the other two if it will help him get away. Each of you needs to be ready for anything." They rode at a trot every eye searching the landscape ahead for the trouble each knew was going to be there...somewhere, anytime. The only question was where and when.

~

Breed knew they were now within five miles of the Border and he begin to feel a little more relaxed. His neck was sore from looking over his shoulder so many times the last few hours looking for that damned scout and the soldiers. They had galloped, trotted, walked, and then galloped their horses for the last ten miles. The horses were laboring now and he knew if the soldiers appeared, a hard run for any distance was out of the question. He knew his life now hung on the chance they could reach the river.

They topped a hill that was a little higher than most and stopped. Each looked at their back trail and they all saw them...maybe a mile behind their present position were the soldiers... and coming fast.

"What are we going to do?" Lupe asked concern showing in his voice. Bill reached up and felt of his throat and thought of a rope around it. Right now he hoped the Breed had some plan.

"We are less than five miles to the river and safety of Mexico. Let's get what we can out of these horses and if they falter, we will find a hole and try to hold them off till dark. There will be no moon tonight so maybe we can get away in the cover of darkness. If your horse goes down grab your canteen before you leave him. He kicked his horse in the flanks and after stumbling the horse took off at an easy gallop. Lupe and Bill followed him.

~

Tye saw the riders when they stupidly sky lined themselves on top of the hill. He figured they were about a mile away. He turned and yelled at the men. "THERE THEY ARE...LETS RIDE," and he jumped from the mount he was on, onto Sandy's back and was off at a dead run. The others did the same with their mounts and were close on Sandy's heels. The ground, covered with low sage and cactus, was a blur to the riders as their horses flew across the land. Tye turned his head and hollered over his shoulder, "Ride loose on the reins so your horse can pick his path." He knew the horses could avert the gopher and prairie dog holes on their on and he and the men could watch for trouble.

"OH GOD!" Lupe screamed as his horse stumbled and then went down throwing him hard to the ground. He quickly stood up and saw Breed and Bill still riding away. "COME BACK...COME BACK!" he screamed. It only took him a second to realize they were not coming back to help him. He cursed them in Spanish and then in English before he took off running. He heard the horses coming behind him. He began running as fast as he could, wondering what made him believe he ever wanted to be a bandito. After close to a hundred yards, the sound of the horses beating the ground was loud and he knew they were close. He stopped, chest heaving, his lungs burning, pulled his gun and turned to meet them.

Gary McMillan

Chapter Fourteen

As Lupe whirled around with his gun in his hand, he was shocked to see a rider almost on top of him. He fired his gun, but knew he had shot too quickly and missed the rider who ducked to the side. He tried to jump out of the way of the huge horse, but it was too late. The horse hit him hard and all the wind went out of him and then he hit the ground and rolled a few times. He sat up and raised his gun hand to fire again at the man but found his hand empty. He lost the grip when he was hit and now he sat on his butt with soldiers and two men dressed as scouts looking down at him. The bigger of the men spoke.

"Private O'Leary, stay with this man till we get back. He tossed him a piece of rawhide. Search him for weapons and then tie his hands behind his back." The big man whirled his horse around and started to leave but stopped. The other man dressed as a scout shouted, "They are down. I saw their horses go down at the same time." The big man looked where the other was pointing and saw the two men scrambling for the rocks about three hundred yards away.

139

The soldier had Lupe's hands tied. This one won't be going anywhere, Tye. Lupe's head came up at the name of Tye. He knew he was looking at the man he wanted to kill…the man who had ended his uncles Alex and Frank's lives. The man called Tye dismounted and walked over to him.

Tye saw he was just a youngster probably no more than twenty years old, if that old. "Little young to be a bandito aren't you, son?" Lupe stared at him with eyes that burned with hate. Tye could see this, felt the hate. "Do you know me…or should I know you?" Lupe said nothing. "If you don't talk, we will consider you part of the gang we were chasing. They are going to hang. You look a little young to be hung, but I guess there have been younger ones before."

Lupe could feel the rope around his neck and he swallowed hard. "My name is Lupe…Lupe Vasquez. I haven't done anything wrong. Those men came into my camp last night."

"Why did you run?"

Lupe lied. He was always a quick thinker. "The older man told me that the troops didn't like Mexicans, and he had come across three that had been hung a couple days ago."

"You looked like you know me or recognized my name a minute ago. Should I know you?"

Before Lupe could think he blurted out, "You killed my uncles, Alex and Frank Vasquez. Tye crossed his arms across his chest, stepped closer and took a good look at the young man. He could see the family resemblance. The Vasquez brothers, along with their band of cutthroats, had robbed a payroll wagon headed to Fort Clark. They, along with some other men, lined the escort up, then shot them one at a time and left them for the buzzards. He had found the men of the escort, or what was left of them after the buzzards had feasted. It was a sight he would never forget.

"So you are kin to Alex and Frank. They were two of the sorriest excuses for men I ever saw."

"Let me tell you how they acquired some of the money. They ambushed a small army payroll escort. They just did not take the money and leave. They lined up the men and shot them one at a time. They rode off and left the men, which I found the next day, to be feasted on by buzzards. There wasn't enough left of most of them to even bury. The food you mentioned, they got from robbing, killing and raping homesteaders around here that wanted nothing else but to be left alone. They must have even robbed your own people, or the Federales would not be looking for them."

Tye stood up. "One more thing you should know, I didn't kill your uncles. The Apaches tortured Frank, and he was near death when I found him. He was staked out with a rattler tied close to his head, and he had been bitten several times. I gave him a gun with one bullet in it…he shot himself. As far as Alex is concerned, I captured him and brought him back for trial. He was found guilty and was hung by the law. I didn't kill them son…they killed themselves by doing what they did against the people. It killed them just like it does eventually for every man that hits the outlaw trail. That's where you are headed unless you change your ways."

"I…I didn't know, I mean…we heard you killed them. My folks, nor any of my village knew what they were doing…I mean we are not dumb. We knew they were stealing maybe…but killing and raping." He hung his head. "I thought I wanted to be like them but now…"

"Cut him loose Private." Tye ordered. O'Riley stepped forward and cut the straps with the big Bowie Tye handed him. Lupe stood there in front of the man he had sworn to kill rubbing his wrist trying to get the circulation back in to them that had been cut off by the rawhide.

"Those men that rode into your camp last night killed a soldier at Fort Inge and then raided a homestead east of here. They shot a fourteen year old boy who survived, killed his mother and father and made off with the boys sixteen year old sister. They had their way with her and then just shot her in the head for no damn reason other than life just don't mean squat to them. They killed another homesteader and his wife after that. Is that the type of people you want to be associated with? Do you have so little value of life that you could kill for no other reason than the fact that you just enjoyed it? Can you honestly look at yourself in the mirror after taking what another man had worked all his life to acquire? If the answer to these questions is no, then go back to your village, get married and have a family like the Lord intended for men to have. If the answer to any of them is yes then here is your gun. Take it and I'll give you an hour's head start before I track you down and bring you in or kill you. The choice is yours."

Tears welled up in the would be outlaw's eyes. He hung his head and in a whispering, breaking voice managed to mumble, "I never thought of it like that. When it came down to it I really don't think I could kill another man unless he was trying to kill me. I guess I was wrong about Uncle Alex and Frank. I guess I was wrong about a lot of things."

"You are a bright young man Lupe Vasquez and you just made the best decision of your life. Hop up behind one of the troopers and we'll get you to the Border and you can go home. Tye reached out his hand and Lupe took it in a firm handshake. He looked up at the big scout.

"I never thought I would being saying this to you...but thanks." He walked over to where O'Riley had mounted his horse. The soldier smiled, reached down with his hand and Lupe grabbed it, the soldier pulled as the youngster jumped and the kid settled in behind the man.

Tye, with Dan beside him, led the others west to where the outlaws had taken refuge.

~

Breed's and Bill's horses stumbled at almost the same time. Both horses managed to stay upright and both men were able to dismount without mishap. They could see the canyon two miles away where the Rio Grande flowed lazily toward the ocean a few hundred miles down river. The river represented safety for the two men…if they could cross it without being shot or caught.

"Let's take our saddles off and put them in that brush over there by that huge mesquite," the Breed said. "We can come back for them later." After hiding the saddles they started walking…and looking over their shoulder. Both men had checked their revolvers and their Henry rifles to make sure they were in working order and loaded.

They had not walked a half a mile when Bill uttered an oath and hollered, "Here they come." Breed looked over his shoulder.

"No way can we outrun them Bill," Breed said. "Let's find a place that we can hole up. It'll be dark in another hour and we can make our way to the river then." They found a place a few minutes later. A jumble of rocks and brush offered protection from the bullets they knew would be coming soon.

Tye was not interested in getting men killed unnecessarily. After the conversation with the young would be outlaw, he led Dan and the three troopers toward the rocks where the two outlaws disappeared. He held the men up about a hundred or so yards from where he figured the men to be. They dismounted and Tye took the binoculars out of his saddle bag. Lying on his belly and raising the glasses to his eyes, he scanned the area all around the rocks the two men were in looking for a way to get close without being seen. Dan lay on his stomach beside Tye. After sweeping the area with the glasses, Tye set the binoculars on the ground.

"Of all the blind luck. Those two's horses played out at the only spot around here that offered no way to sneak up on the men."

"You know they will try to make it to the Border after dark," Dan said.

"Yeah, I know that. It's going to be up to you and me to see they don't."

"You have a plan?" Dan asked.

Tye shook his head. "Not yet, but between you and me, we will figure something out." He looked over his shoulder where the men stood, holding the reins of all their mounts. "Slip back to the men and tell them to picket their horses and make themselves comfortable till we get us a plan together." Tye lay there resting his chin on his forearms thinking about what they should do other than just charge the rocks and probably get half of the men killed. He thought about his pa and things he had told him.

When you are tracking men or in a dangerous situation and are at a point you don't know what to do or what the men you are after are going to do...put yourself in their place. Ask yourself what you would do if you were them. You will be surprised how many times you will be right.

Tye thought about what he would do if he was Breed. I would know the soldiers would think I am going straight to the Border after dark and they would put men between where we are and the river. I could go to the south or north of where I am instead of due west where they figure I will be. By going south or north for maybe a half a mile and then going toward the Border I might just pass them by.

Tye went back to where the men were. "This is what we are going to do. The obvious thing for those two to do would be to head to the border after full dark. They probably know we know that and we would have men west of them to prevent that." He picked up a twig and drew two "x's" in the dirt. "This mark is us and that mark is them." He drew a crooked line about a foot from the "x" marking the two men's location. "That is the river and the Border. I think they will try to outsmart us and go right or left from where they are instead of directly toward the Border. They will think they can get around us, so this is what we will do."

Tye looked at Dan. "Just before dark take O'Riley and Washington and get to the south of the rocks. Spread out so they can't get around you. I'll take Langley here and cover the north side."

"What happens," Dan asked, "If they ain't smart enough to think we will be between them and the river and just head straight for it?"

"The Breed is smart. He hasn't evaded the law and the army for all this time by being stupid, but if I'm wrong then you and I will take a trip into Mexico while the men go back to Clark. But, I think he will figure we are directly between him and the river and won't go that way."

I hope you are right because I have no desire to go to Mexico to chase them or for any other reason," Dan said smiling.

Only half of the sun was above the western hills. Tye loved this time of day and would sometimes just sit and look at the sunsets and wonder how anyone could not believe there was not a God above. There had to be to make something as pretty as a Texas sunset. "It will be dark enough to move into position in a few minutes so get your men together. We'll picket the horses over yonder," he said pointing with the Henry in his hand, "In that grove of mesquites." The soldiers followed the two scouts, took care of their mounts and then gathered around the two men. They understood the plan and were anxious to carry it out and get this patrol over with. The beer at Jim's Saloon was beckoning them and they were anxious to get back for that if for no other reason. The two groups left to take up positions... and wait.

Waiting...Tye knew that was the worse part of being a soldier on patrol. You know something is going to happen and men are probably going to die. At times like this, a man sometimes has too much time to mediate, to think about things. He will reflect on his life and what he has done, didn't do, or should have done. If he is married he thinks of his loved ones...will I see them again and did I tell them how much they mean to me before I left? Thoughts like these can make his insides be tied up in knots, make him anxious and worse of all...lose his nerve.

Tye thought he had seen this in the men's faces when they went to their positions. They were young, inexperienced soldiers and he expected nothing less from them. Even old veteran soldiers had these same looks before going into a battle. Most of them would handle it the way they should and perform their duty but a few would not. Having ridden with these men and the way he prided himself in knowing men, he thought these would do fine.

He hoped he was right about what the two men would do. Like Dan, he had rather not go into Mexico. There were no friends over there: just Apache, poor people who hate the Texans, Bandits who would try to rob and kill them, and worse of all...the Federales. I want to end this thing here and now; he thought.

Time passed slowly as it always does at times like this. Tye, looking at the stars, figured it was after ten and he thought maybe he had guessed wrong. The thought had no sooner crossed his mind when a shout and a shot sounded at the same time from where Dan was. "Stay here," he whispered to Langley. "Be careful you don't shoot one of our men...or me." He patted the private on the shoulder and disappeared in the darkness.

Gary McMillan

Chapter Fifteen

Tye heard a sound like a muffled cry to his left and made his way toward it. After three or four steps he stopped to listen. He heard it again much closer to him this time. Three more silent steps and he found the source...Private O'Riley lay on his back with blood oozing between his fingers from a wound he was holding his hands over in his belly. Tye whirled when a voice spoke a few feet from him.

"It's me Tye,...Dan." The scout moved to where Tye was kneeling over the soldier. "Is it bad?" he asked.

"Knife wound...has to be that damn Breed," Tye whispered. "He wears those moccasin boots like us so he will be hard to hear when he's moving. They are moving slow or we would have heard them. Move to my left a few feet and let's see if we can find them." They moved slowly with only a couple steps separating them, their eyes straining in the darkness, ears tuned for any sound, nerves on a razor edge. They had their revolvers in their left hands and their Bowie knifes in their right as they

151

moved slowly one step at a time, stopped and listened, and moved again. Sweat rolled down the men's faces as much from the tension as from the warm nighttime temperature.

A scream shattered the still night air and Tye and Dan froze. A shot sounded just ahead of them and then a voice. "Damn you to hell, Bill," they heard a man say which they figured to be the Breed. The voice was followed by a scream…then silence. The two scouts waited. They knew where the sounds come from so Tye hollered.

"Stay where you are Washington; you too Langley. Don't neither of you move."
The two scouts moved quickly and silently over the rocky ground, the only sound was the moaning they could hear in front and to the right of them. The sound was like a beacon and they headed straight for it.

They found Bill, who like O'Riley, had been stabbed. They also found the reason for the shot…a huge rattlesnake lay two feet from Bill with its head blown off.

Tye knelt down beside the outlaw and saw the wound was fatal. He had been stabbed in the left lung and blood was being coughed up by the man. Bill opened his eyes and looked at Tye. "Yo..you Wa…Watkins?" he asked, his words barely audible.

Tye nodded, "I'm Watkins."

"Is my brother and nephew still alive?" he asked struggling now for breaths between his words.

"They are with the other soldiers on their way back to Fort Inge. What happened?"

Bill gasped a couple times and choked on the blood that was coming from his lungs with every breath and trickled from the corner of his mouth. "I stepped on that rattler an…and h…he bit me in the leg." He coughed and a large amount of blood bubbled from the corners of his mouth. "The Breed, he stab…," he gasped one more time and died before he could finish.

Tye leaned close to Dan and whispered, "I think we might as well wait till its light, and maybe we can pick up the Breed's trail. He can hide and with us moving through the brush and just might knife another one of us."

The scouts backtracked and found Washington and Langley. The two privates brought the severely wounded O'Riley to where the scouts were and made him as comfortable as possible. Tye tore the shirt open and inspected the wound. He looked up at Dan and the scout shook his head. Tye nodded his understanding that it was a fatal wound. It might not have been fatal with a surgeon and a hospital close by but out here…it was unless they could get him to the fort quick…damn quick.

"How quick could you get to the fort Dan?" Tye asked

"You're not thinking of taking on the Breed by yourself are you?"

"O'Riley ain't going to make it if we don't get him some medical help. Besides, I have Washington and Langley."

"I don't think he'll make it anyway," Dan said.

"Maybe not," Tye replied, "But can you look at yourself in the mirror if we don't give him a chance?"

Dan nodded. "With him in the shape he is in…maybe four or five hours."

"Let's get a travois put together and you head out with him.

"What is a travois?" Washington asked.

"You seen the Indians pulling two poles with a blanket stretched between to form a bed?" Dan asked.

"Yes sir."

"That's a travois," Dan said. The private nodded his understanding.

"I 've seen you and Tye make them before for different wounded men but I didn't know that was what it was called," Washington said. They wrapped O'Riley's wound as tightly as possible and lay the soldier in the travois with a canteen. Tye instructed him not to swallow the water but just rinse his mouth and spit it out. Dan left for Clark and Tye sat down with the two privates to wait for daylight.

Breed, when he figured out the soldiers were not looking for him, made his way through the brush heading for the river a mile or so away. He wasn't moving fast because he was thinking two things, rattlesnakes and leaving as few tracks as possible. He had hated to kill Bill, but he wasn't going to do anything but slow him down after being bit by the snake. Besides it was stupid for Bill to have screamed like a damn woman when he got bit and then fired his pistol and let everyone within a mile know where they were.

He had walked about two hundred yards when he almost stepped on another rattler. He would have if he had not been warned by the unforgettable rattling of the snake shaking his tail. A little shook up at coming that close to being bit he circled the snake and decided to wait till he could see before moving again. He figured he had about four hours to wait.

Tye sat with the men for a few minutes then stood up and walked over to Sandy. They kept the horses in close for two reasons: to keep Breed from stealing them and also they could hear them whinny, snort, and generally make a lot of noise if anything or anyone came close to camp. Tye had some thinking to do and he wanted to be alone doing it. He stood beside Sandy scratching him under the chin while staring into the darkness toward the river thinking things over.

155

There's two choices he was thinking: one, I can wait till daylight and then chase him into Mexico because he will beat us to the Border, or two, I can try and beat him by going now and maybe catch him at the river. There's a hill I am familiar with that I could see a long ways up and down the river. With the glasses I could spot him coming and maybe set a trap for him.

The problem is the snakes. This particular part of the country is over populated with them, some of them six feet long or longer, and some as big around as a man's upper leg. Some say the large number is because of the great number of small varmints that live in this area like the ground squirrel, prairie dogs, rabbits, and even some birds that spend a lot of time on the ground like the quail. Whatever the reason, a man moving at night had better be careful. The devils hole up during the heat of the day and do their hunting in the coolness of the night. He mulled these things over and made the decision it was worth the risk.

He walked back to where the two soldiers waited. "If we don't get to the river before Breed, I'll end up going all over Mexico trying to find him so I think the thing to do is try and beat him there and catch him before he crosses. Do either of you have any questions or ideas? The two looked at each other and shrugged.

"We're with you Tye," Washington said.

"What about the horses?" Langley asked.

"One of you will have to stay here and watch them. That damn sneaky varmint could decide to circle back and try to get them. You two decide between you who will stay and who will go with me."

"Why don't you go? I'll watch the horses," Washington said. Langley nodded and picked up his Sharps.

"I'm ready when you are Tye."

Tye looked at Washington. "Don't go to sleep. Keep your eyes on Sandy. If his ears perk up and start twitching, be ready because something or someone is close by."

"I understand," Washington said nodding his head.

"Let's go then," he said to Langley. "Walk right behind me and listen for any unusual sounds."

They had walked about a hundred yards when they heard it...the unmistakable sound of a rattler giving his warning buzz. Both men stopped in their tracks and listened, trying to locate where the sound was coming from. In the dark, the sound sounded like it was all around them. To help locate the sound Tye held his Henry rifle by the barrel and leaned forward as he swept the area in front and to both sides of him with the stock.

On the second sweep the pitch of the rattlers buzzing increased indicating to Tye he was close to the deadly reptile. They circled to the left around the snake was and headed on toward the river.

Sweat poured off Langley even though the early morning air was still cool. He knew better than to say anything because a man's voice can carry a long ways on a still night like this, but he was scared…dirty your pants kind of scared. He hated snakes and had since that day on a hill when he was a young boy. A boyhood friend of his had fallen into a den of the serpents when he was eleven years old and died because of all the bites. He had never forgotten the screams of his friend. An Apache warrior he could handle, but he wanted no part of a damn rattlesnake.

They moved slowly and quietly with Tye raking the area in front of them with the Henry before each step. No more snakes were found and an hour before first light Tye found the hill he was looking for. They climbed to the top and then lay on the west side which was opposite the side Breed would be coming from. They would be looking east on the backside of the hill from the approaching Breed so they should not be visible to the outlaw.

Tye figured there was an hour before the grayness of the morning replaced the inky blackness they were in now. Tye knew it was always the darkest a little before dawn because if there had been a moon it would be down and the night time stars would be gone also. He prayed he had guessed right that Breed had decided to hole up till first light. If he didn't, he was already in Mexico. He hoped Washington stayed alert too because he would be no match for the Breed if the outlaw did try to get the horses. He was thinking there was a lot of, if this and if that...too many. He figured they were as ready as they ever would be, so his mind drifted to something else ...Rebecca.

He loved her with all his heart, but the moment she said she was with child that love took on a whole new meaning. He remembered his pa telling him that   the proudest moment in a man's life was the instant his baby was born. The second greatest thing in a man's life was watching that youngster grow up and into a human being that he could be proud of. He would make sure that his child had the same love and guidance that he had received. His thoughts of seeing Rebecca with their child in her arms brought a lump to his throat.

His thoughts of Rebecca were interrupted by Langley's elbow nudging him. Langley was pointing to the left. Tye shifted his eyes and through the early morning dim light saw something moving a couple hundred yards away. He slowly raised his field glasses to his eyes knowing a fighting man would notice sudden and quick movements more easily than slow deliberate ones. The Breed was a fighting man and Tye wanted to give him no breaks if he could help it. After a couple of seconds searching the area Tye was able to spot the source of movement...it was the Breed. His heart jumped a beat and a whole lot of worry left him as he watched the man. Even if Tye did not know the man was part Apache, he would have guessed it just by the way the man moved and by the way he was ever watchful of things around him. As he watched, the Breed swung slightly to his left and walked toward the hill...straight at where Tye and Langley lay.

Chapter Sixteen

Tye watched the man coming toward them and knew what was going to happen. He knew the Breed, being part Apache, would spot the boot prints of Langley. As he watched, he saw the man stop, look at the ground and immediately drop behind a thick sage bush.

"What did he do that for?" Langley whispered.

"He saw your boot tracks and knows we are up here."

"Damn!"

Damn is right Tye thought? I figure now we are going to play a game that no one was better at than the Apache...the waiting game. This was a game in which the man who moved first could be the last move he ever made. Tye knew patience was taught to an Apache from the time he was old enough to learn to track and hunt, which was about the age of four or five.

"Don't take your eyes off that sage, Langley. If you see anything move ...shoot."

"Where are you going?" Langley asked his face expressing concern.

"Down this hill and see if I flank him and flush him out."

"You be careful Tye."

Tye smiled and patted the private on the shoulder. "Always am," he said as he scooted down the slope a few feet, got to his feet, and in a crouch shuffled down the hill. Reaching bottom, he turned and moved quickly to his right and dropped into a ravine.

A minute later he knew he had made a mistake. The ravine, maybe four foot deep, ran along the base of the hill and turned east…just at the base of the sage the Breed ducked behind. He glanced down at the sandy bottom of the ravine where he stood. He was looking for tracks and seeing none he ran to the bush where the Breed disappeared behind. He glanced up and saw Langley wave at him. Tye was going to warn him that the outlaw may be on his left flank but he didn't get the words out. A shot rang out and Tye heard the all too familiar thump of a bullet hitting flesh. Langley screamed, and as Tye watched the private roll on his side and then tumble a few feet down the steep slope of the hill toward Tye. Tye, cussing under his breath, climbed out of the ravine and scrambled to the top of the hill. Looking over, he just got a glimpse of Breed as he disappeared over the rim of the bank of the river about a hundred yards away. Tye stumbled, slid, and ran down the other side intending to get a shot at him. Reaching the bottom of the hill, he ran as hard as he could, dodging cactus, boulders, and leaping a couple of narrow ravines. He reached the rim out of breath and saw the Breed a little over a hundred yards away. He had already crossed the narrow, knee-deep Rio Grande and was now in Mexico. The outlaw stopped, turned and looking back saw Tye and waved at him. Tye knew the distance was too great for the Henry for any accuracy. He wished he had his Sharps with its much longer range. He fired four shots at the man and saw the bullets hitting the water and mud of the far bank, short of where Breed stood. He raised the rifle again and aiming over Breed's head, fired again. The waving stopped as the Breed grabbed his left arm, staggered a bit, turned around and ran around a large mesquite and out of sight.

At least I nicked him and probably scared the hell out of him, Tye thought. I had better get back to Langley and check on him before chasing that bastard into Mexico.

He found Langley and was relieved he was alive. He had been hit in the shoulder and the bullet had passed through cleanly. He would be fine but was going to be in a world of hurt for a few hours till he got back to the fort and old sawbones. He took the private's kerchief off and plugged the hole in the front of his shoulder and then picked him up, threw him over his shoulder and headed toward Private Washington and the horses.

163

When he was close to the spot he had left Washington, he hollered. WASHINGTON, THIS IS TYE, I'M COMING IN."

A nervous Washington had never been so glad to hear a man's voice in his life. He had been a nervous wreck since Tye and Langley left. He was alone and if something happed to his buddy's, he hadn't a clue as to how to get back to the fort. Since leaving Fort Clark they had turned, circled, and back-tracked so many times he wasn't even sure which direction he was facing now. And the land, hell, it all looked the same. There were no outstanding landmarks to go by. He, Langley and some of the others were always amazed by men like Tye that seemed to travel through this country and arrived where they wanted to be like they had been traveling on a road…with a map showing them the way.

He laid his rifle on the saddle when he saw Tye with Langley over his shoulder, and ran to meet him. "Is…is he dead?" He asked, genuine concern showing for his friend.

"No," Tye said. "He's hit in the shoulder and will be fine." With Washington's help, they gently laid the wounded man on a blanket. "I'm going to wrap his arm tight to his chest and you take him to the fort as fast as you can. You should be there before nightfall."

"Tye, I don't know…I don't know how to find the fort," an excited, obviously nervous Washington replied.

Tye smiled. "All you have to do Private is head north," he said pointing with his finger. "Keep the sun on your right till it's overhead and then on your left as it goes down. You will hit the Old mail Road and go right. It will take you to the fort." He waited for an answer. "Understand what I said?" The private nodded his head. "You give Langley some water and clean his face some." Again Washington just nodded.

In a few short minutes Tye had the arm tight against Langley's chest. Together they picked up the soldier and put him on his horse with Langley cussing them with every breath.

"Head north and remember what I told you about the sun. You will have no trouble finding the road. I figure at the pace you will be traveling you should reach the road a little after mid-afternoon. You won't be far from the fort. After you take him to see old sawbones, report to Thurston and tell him I'm in Mexico after Breed.

"Yes, Sir." Washington answered.

Tye put his hand on the shoulder of the soldier. "You'll be fine Private. Just get Langley there as fast as you can." Washington mounted his horse and Tye handed him the reins of Langley's horse. Washington and Tye's eyes locked on each other. Tye gave him a smile and said, "Get moving." For the first time Washington smiled back, nodded and headed north, leading the horse with his friend. Tye watched for a moment, then walked over and took a piece of jerky out of his saddle bag and stuck the end in his mouth. He picked up the saddle and put it on Sandy. He mounted and sat there, chewed the jerky and washed it down with some warm water from his canteen.

I had best not forget to get water from the river because there's no telling when I will find more over there. Where the Breed went, I'm not familiar with that part of Mexico other than it's known as Terreno Desconocido-the unknown land. I heard it was an arid and dreary place that few people lived in. It was a trackless desert bounded by mountains. I know this, if I don't catch him quick, some unfortunate Mexicans he might stumble onto will be dead.

He gently nudged Sandy with the heels of his moccasin boots and headed toward the river and Mexico. When he reached the rive he dismounted and let Sandy drink his fill. He took a spare canteen he carried from his saddle bag and filled it as well as the one hanging from his saddle. He sat on his haunches, butt resting on his heels, and took a long drink and then refilled the canteen to the brim. Sandy had quit sucking up the water so Tye remounted and him take them across the Rio Grande, into Mexico and to what ever fate had in store for him.

166

Chapter Seventeen

Tye found Breed's tracks as soon as Sandy's hooves hit the Mexican soil. He also saw blood on some cane that the man had ran through. On the other side of the stand of cane, Tye found tracks showing the outlaw was walking. Tye smiled.

Breed thinks he's safe because we won't follow him over here. That's going to work in my favor because with him thinking like that he won't be working hard to cover his tracks plus I might just catch him by surprise.

It had rained in the last twenty-four hours by the appearance of the land. The ever present dust was not on the plants and a few small puddles of water stood in some of the low, rocky pockets. The tracks were easy to follow and Tye, leery of the Breed's ability from his Apache upbringing was watchful. A fighting man like Breed could sometimes feel he is being watched or followed. Tye was walking, leading Sandy instead of riding, all his senses alert . He held the reins in his left hand, the Henry in his right...thumb on the hammer. He was less than a half hour behind the man so he decided to find a place to leave Sandy. It didn't take long. A shady spot along a small cliff that had a pool of water was perfect. He hobbled Sandy and scratched him between the ears. "I'll be back soon ole boy." Sandy nodded his head bringing a smile to Tye's face. He always told people that his horse understood everything he said.

Breed was sitting on a large flat rock wrapping the wound on his left arm with the sleeve of his shirt he had torn off. The bullet had torn through the inside of his forearm, just below the elbow. No bones were hit and had it had just about quit bleeding. The wrap was put on to keep dirt out which he hoped would keep it from becoming infected.

What I need is some whiskey...a little to pour on the wound and a lot to drink. That damn scout is either the best damn shot I ever saw, or the luckiest. I think maybe it was a good shot. I think maybe that scout is as good as I have heard, but that don't matter now, he's over there and I'm over here and I don't intend to go back...at least for awhile. I don't think I will find anyone in the desert that I can get some food or a horse from so I think it's best to travel along the bank of the river. There should be some people living there.

He stood up and made his way north, staying a quarter of a mile from the river. He had not walked a mile when he saw some goats. He knew where there were goats; there would be a house nearby. He sat down out of sight to watch and see if anyone appeared. He checked his arm and saw that the bleeding had stopped. He sat in the shade of a giant mesquite, his back against a smooth rock and waited.

Tye studied the vague foot prints of the Breed's moccasin boots and had some thoughts on the way things were.

I'm close...real close. You'd be damn smart ole boy to keep your eyes open and move real slow and careful. He probably doesn't have a clue I'm anywhere this side of the river, but he's going to be careful anyway.

He stood up and with his eyes followed the path the man was taking. That is when he saw the goats. He dropped behind a large boulder and took his hat off and studied the surrounding terrain. He knew if the Breed saw the goats he would be watching for the herder to show up. That someone would be dead soon after that and that was what Tye knew he had to prevent from occurring.

He started to change positions when he saw the man coming from the other side of the goats. He was a small man and wore the white pants and shirt that was so prevalent in Mexico. Tye saw he had apparently had no weapon other than a wooden stick. Tye stayed where he was and waited to see if Breed showed his hand. The Mexican sat down near the goats. Tye waited.

169

His patience paid off. He saw the Mexican stand up quickly and look to his left. Tye looked where the man was looking and he saw him...the Breed. He was walking toward the Mexican, who Tye could see wasn't sure what to do...run like hell or wait and see what the stranger wanted. He waited.

Tye was no more than forty yards from the Mexican whose back was slightly toward him as he watched the Breed approach. Tye eased the Henry to his shoulder and shifted his body to where he was comfortable and ready to shoot if it looked like the Breed was going to harm the man. He didn't like the idea of shooting a man from ambush, but he was not going to let Breed kill the man. He had the sights of the rifle square on the Breed's chest and his finger on the trigger. He heard them as they started talking.

Breed spoke first. "Speak English, Hombre?

"Si...I speak a little English.

"Good," Breed said as he stopped in front of the man who was looking the stranger over.

"What happened?" he asked pointing to Breed's arm.

"Bandito's." Breed answered. "They shot my horse and after I shot one of them, I guess they figured I wasn't worth the trouble. They rode off." He looked where the Mexican had come from but saw no house. "You live close by?"

"Si. I live about a half mile over there," he said pointing with his hand. "There is a small village just past it."

"Anyone have a horse for sale?"

"We are all poor, senor. Most do not own a horse but those who do, like me, use them for work, not riding. They are not what a man such as you would want."

"And just what kind of man do you think I am?" Breed asked, his words having an edge to them.

The Mexican shrugged his shoulders. "I don't know you, senor, but I would guess maybe a pistoleer," he said pointing to the gun on Breed's hip.

"Me?" The Breed said sounding as innocent as he could be. "A pistoleer? I'm a ranch hand that came over here for some fun with the senoritas… until those bandits tried to rob me."

The Mexican had already noticed the Breed's smooth hands. "Your hands do not look like you have done much work, senor."

"Damn guy is pretty sharp", Tye muttered under his breath. "But he had better watch his mouth around Breed. He blinked and was surprised to see a pistol materialize in the Breed's hand.

"You mouth just got you in a lot of trouble, Mexican," he said holding the pistol not a foot from the man's chest.

Tye stood up and hollered. "DROP YOUR GUN BREED!" The Breed's head snapped around and saw he was a dead man if he made the wrong move. He remembered the shot this man

171

made at the river. He dropped the gun and Tye walked toward him holding the Henry pointed at the outlaw.

"Who are you?" the Mexican asked, looking at Tye.

"Tye Watkins," Tye answered now within ten yards of the men.

"I have heard of you. What are you doing over here?"

"Chasing this man," Tye said. "He is wanted for murder, rape, and stealing. His name is Miguel Espinosa but most people know him as the Breed."

The Mexican turned toward Tye and took a step that placed him almost between Tye and the Breed. Before Tye could tell him not to get between them, Breed made his move.

"I have heard of h..." his words were cut off by the Breeds wounded arm around his neck, and a knife's point touching his cheek. Tye was surprised by the quick move.

"Drop the rifle Watkins," he ordered. Tye saw the fear in the Mexican's face. He dropped the rifle. "Now your Navy Colt and do it slowly." Tye obeyed. The Breed looked Tye up and down for more weapons but he was on Tye's left and could not see the Bowie in his right boot. He shoved the Mexican toward Tye and this was what Tye was waiting for.

Reaching down he pulled the Bowie, pushed the Mexican aside and stepped toward the Breed. 'Now," he said. "It's just you and me, Breed...and these," he said waving the ten inch

Bowie in front of Breed. Breed looked at his knife and it was half the size of Tye's. He knew he was going to hang if he went back to Texas so…he swung wildly at Tye with his knife and then swung again at Tye's midsection as the scout was forced to backpedal from the furious onslaught.

Once again the wild slashes came as Tye continued moving back and to his left. As he moved he studied the Breed's attack and the next time he was ready. He stepped back and as the knife passed his belly he stepped forward with his left foot and kicked viciously at the Breed's knee with his right. His foot connected solidly with the outlaw's right knee, and a loud howl emitted from the Breed as his right leg collapsed under him. He fell on his side and grabbed his knee, his knife forgotten. He had been stabbed and shot before, but neither hurt like this. Holding his knee, he rolled on the ground cursing Tye with every breath.

Tye squatted down beside him and smiled. The Mexican came up just as Tye spoke to the half-breed. "The pain will begin to go away in a minute Breed, but you are going to be limping around some for awhile. We will take up the fight again in a few minutes when you feel better."

Breed's head jerked up and looked at Tye. "You want to continue the fight?"

"Breed, that family you and your friends murdered, and the girl you raped and then killed were relatives of mine. I intend to see you pay…pay with a hell of a lot of pain before you hang."

"Yo…You can't do that," the Breed stammered out. "You are not even supposed to even be over here!"

"But I am Breed…over here. And you…you are fixing to be in more hurt than you ever imagined. Tye stood up and kicked him in the chest knocking him on his back…into a small patch of cactus. Another scream came from deep in the Breed's throat. He rolled on to his side and sat up. He tried to reach the thorns between his shoulder blades with his good right arm but could not.

"Stand up Breed," Tye ordered.

"STAND UP HELL! I CAN'T," Breed screamed.

"You'll stand up," Tye said calmly, "or I will kill you where you sit you worthless piece of horse shit." He jerked the man to his feet and bending over, picked up the dropped knife and placed it in the outlaw's right hand and quickly stepped back.

"You have the knife Breed…use it…kill me." Breed, in a daze because of the pain, looked at the knife and quickly dropped it.

"No," he said, his face grimacing with the pain in his knee and the thorns in his back.

"In that case…" Tye hit him in the belly with a right fist that doubled the man over and then caught him flush in the face with a knee that rocked his head back. He collapsed…out cold.

The Mexican bent over the prostrate body of Breed. "He is really the outlaw, Miguel Espinosa?"

Tye nodded. "That's him," he sighed, the anger in him stemming a little. He was glad the man was out because he would have killed him for no reason other than hate.

That would be something I have never done…killed because of hate. I could though…images of the murdered couple, the dead girl, and the boy who had lost everything appeared. Damn him to hell.

Tye looked at the Mexican and for the first time realized he was much older than he had thought…maybe in his fifties. Then again, this land beat a man down and sometimes they looked older than they were.

He remembered his good friends the Turley's, with whom he had spent time with in his younger years. They were his pa and ma's best friends and closest neighbor. They were killed a little over a year ago by Tanza and his band of renegades and the warrior took their grandchildren captive. Tye tracked Tanza down and killed him, and brought the children back to Fort Clark where they were taken in by the O'Malleys. Tye could still see the faces of the Turleys and

175

he had always thought them to be old. He was shocked the day his ma told him they were only four or five years older than his pa. His pa explained to him that was what long hours under the Texas sun could do to man's skin. Add the strain of always being on the razor edge of life and death every time a rider approached, the bandits roaming around, plus the Apaches...he could have gone on and on but I understood. I also knew I probably could not guess within ten years this man's age.

"This man...this dog of a man killed a good friend of mine two years ago," the Mexican said. "He knifed him in the belly and left him to die. My friend crawled on his belly almost a mile before he died... less than fifty yards from his hacienda and his wife and two children. The two men had had an argument in a cantina earlier that night and this dog killed him as he walked home." He looked down and spit on the man.

Tye liked this man. "Well, he's not killing anyone else." He knelt down and rolled Breed onto his stomach. He grabbed the man's hands and tied them securely behind his back, not being too careful as to whether they were to tight. He pulled what thorns he could out of the man's back but several were still there that would have to fester before coming out.

176

Tye smiled at his Mexican friend. "He's going be in some pain for awhile with that broke knee and his back full of thorns, and then about the time he's feeling better, he'll hang."

"He is part Apache," the Mexican said. "You must take care on your trip back to Fort Clark. He is a dangerous, desperate man. I can go and help."

"I know that but he's not going to be able to do much for a few days and he'll be in the guardhouse by this time tomorrow. Thanks for your offer though."

"Thank you Senor. I think maybe I would be dead if you had not shown up when you did. My village is just over there," pointing with the stick. "The least I can do for saving my life is offering you something good to eat."

Tye nodded and shook the man's hand. "I appreciate the offer. By the way, we haven't officially met. You know my name but I don't know yours." The Mexican smiled.

"Pequeno LozanoAlamendarez."

Tye grinned. "That's quite a mouthful."

"My father had a fondness for names," the man said laughing. "My friends call me Pablo."

"Pablo it is then," Tye said as he reached down and grabbed the back of Breed's collar, jerked the man to his feet and while holding him upright, slapped his face a few times to wake him up. A groan from Breed was the first indication he was regaining consciousness. Tye released his grip on the man's collar and Breed staggered, almost falling down before regaining his balance.

"Let's go Breed," Tye ordered. "We have a walk ahead of us."

"WALK! You broke my damn knee. I can't walk."

"We are going to this man's village and YOU WILL WALK," Tye said his voice rising in anger. Breed cursed him again, and slowly shuffled after the Mexican.

"My father knew your father," Pablo said as they walked. Tye looked at the man. "He used to visit your home. He thought a lot of your father…said he was an honorable man."

"Your father's name Horatio?"

"Si, Senor. That was a long time ago."

"I remember him. He came to our home several times. I was very young, but I remember him being a very nice man and my father liked him very much."

Tye remembered the man. He was always dressed immaculately and had very good manners, especially when his mother was around. He remembered his being fascinated with the horse the man rode. It was as black as the night and his saddle and breast collar had a great number of silver coins on them. His pa always said the man to be well off and owed a lot of land across the river.

"He was a great man…an important man for many years. Crooked officials and soldiers took his land. They killed him one night as he rode home after trying to get the president, who was a friend of his, to help. It turned out the president was helping the ones who took his land."

"I have heard of such goings on over there. I'm sorry. Is your mother still alive?"

"Si, but she is in very bad health."

"Sorry to hear that. Pablo, if there is ever a way I can help you and your family, you just let me know," Tye said putting his hand on the man's shoulder. Pablo nodded.

Arriving at the village, the first thing Tye noticed were the kids playing and the dogs running around with them. He smiled.

This is not what I expected. I figured a village that was poor, dirty, and starving. The houses were not mansions, but they were neat and laid out in rows. Several women were washing clothes in what appeared to be a large spring. He saw no young men, only a few old ones who were sitting under a tree at a table talking. He also noticed that all the playing, washing of clothes and talking stopped when he entered the village. It wasn't everyday gringos came to visit. Pablo spoke very loud in Spanish telling everyone that I was his friend and had saved him from this bandito. He did not mention Breed's name.

179

A woman came up to Pablo and he spoke in Spanish. She nodded and went into a house. "Let's sit over here," Pablo said walking into the shade of one of the houses. As they sat down the woman came out of the house with a plate of tortillas, beans, and a picture of water and cups. Tye took one bite and then began eating in earnest as his taste buds told him this was damn good. He noticed Breed wasn't letting the food sit long on his plate either.

After eating, Tye thanked Pablo and said he needed to get going. They had a lot of miles to cover.

"You will always be welcome here my friend." He reached out and shook Tye's hand. Tye nodded and turned to Breed.

"Let's go." He looked over his shoulder at Pablo. "Remember what I said about helping." Pablo smiled broadly showing a mouth full of teeth and nodded.

"I think I would like to stay here," Breed said smiling.

"Then stay here. That Mexican over there and some of his friends would like that. Seems you killed a good friend of theirs. I hear they can get pretty vicious with those big machete knives they carry sometimes."

Breed looked at the Mexicans and shrugged his shoulders. "I'll go with you."

Chapter Eighteen

Thirty minutes later, Tye sat on Sandy on the Texas side of the Rio Grande. Breed had made it across the river but had cursed Tye in Spanish, Apache, and English, every step of the way. Tye knew the man was in pain and while listening to his ranting, just smiled...then something his pa told him a long time ago made him think about what he was doing.

Scouting for the army and tracking men is dangerous enough without letting personal feelings come into play. By letting that happen, your judgment could be affected. Same thing can happen with anger. You do your best when you are calm and simply concentrating on the job at hand. Also it was not your job to judge a man...simply bring him in and let the courts judge them. God will issue final judgment.

Tye looked at Breed and then at the sky, the hills...looking, but not really seeing anything. He wanted this bastard to suffer, but what his pa said long ago kept coming back. "Damn," he

181

said and dismounted. "Sit over there," he said to Breed, pointing to a small shaded area under a mesquite. "Don't you move an inch," he said, in a tone that Breed knew he meant it. Tye looked around for material to build a travois. It only took him a few minutes, and he had the poles strapped to the saddle on Sandy and placed Breed on it. Breed was relieved when Tye took off the rawhide strips that bound his wrist, and he was thinking this was careless of a man like Tye. That thought ended quickly when Tye lashed his wrists to the poles on each side of the travois. Then his feet were tied together.

"Bastard," he muttered just loud enough for Tye to hear.

"You say one more word Breed, and I swear you will walk every step of the way to the Fort, and I won't care how much you are hurting. If you fall down, I'll put a rope on you and drag you the rest of the way." Breed started to say something but decided it was to his best interest to say nothing. He bit his lip and lay his head back on the blanket. Tye mounted Sandy and they headed toward Fort Clark. Every minute or so Tye looked behind him, checking on Breed making sure he was still secure.

Night was coming and Tye was searching for a place to camp. He hadn't heard a word from Breed for over an hour and that was just to inform his captor he needed to relieve his bladder. Tye told him to hold it for awhile.

The sun had just disappeared behind the hills when the scout found what he was looking for. A couple of big oak trees would offer the perfect place. There was a little grama grass for Sandy to munch on and the thick trunk of one of the oaks would be perfect to tie Breed to and not have to lose sleep worrying about him escaping.

After letting his prisoner take care of his personal business, Tye held a gun on him while the man ate some jerky. Tye allowed him to drink some water and then had him sit facing the trunk of an oak. He then had him slide up to the trunk and straddle it. Tye then tied his hands and feet on the other side of the trunk. He started to walk away but turned back and smiling, said. "Now don't you go and get too comfortable."

Tye lay down on his blanket with his head resting on his saddle which served as a pillow. As he lay there, he looked up through the branches of the oak tree he lay under at God's masterpiece…the Texas sky. There was no moon and only a few stars at this time of night but in thirty or so minutes there would be a million of them. The only sound in the still blackness that surrounded him was Sandy munching grass a few feet away. He was exhausted from the strain of the last twenty-four hours. The last thing he remembered was the lonely wailing of a coyote.

Tye woke up from a deep sleep and for a second he could not remember where he was…but only for a second. He lay there looking at the night sky which was clear when he went to sleep, but now clouds covered the stars and lightning flashed over the western hills.

That's all I need right now…rain. Without the stars, I am not sure exactly what time it was but figure I have been asleep four or five hours which would make it about three o'clock. Pa taught me to tell time by the position of the stars, but he didn't tell me how to when there were none. That thought brought a smile.

Tye walked over to Breed and lightly kicked him in the butt. "Wake up. We're moving out, Breed."

"I don't think I can move after being in this position you had me in for all these hours you…." He thought better of cussing Tye again. Tye smiled. He remembered another outlaw that had cursed him every breath he took. Yancey Cates was still cussing him the day he was hung. Tye knew Breed was hurting something fierce. The outlaws knee was swollen and stretching his pants, the bullet wound in his arm probably burned like the dickens, and he was sure those thorns in the man's back were festering.

Tye untied the Breed's hands and feet. "Get up," he ordered.

"You're gonna have to help me."

"I don't think so," Tye replied. He was not going to give the man any chance to get the upper hand by placing himself that close. He knew the man was hurting, but he also knew he was desperate, and desperate men are dangerous. "NOW GET YOUR ASS UP," he placed his right foot on the injured knee and put just a little weight on it bringing a groan from Breed. "You going to get up?"

Breed cursed him and very slowly stood up, almost falling when he tried to put weight on his right leg. He cursed again.

"Get over there on the travois," Tye said. "Walk, crawl, or fly, I don't care, but get your butt over there now."

Breed took a step with his right leg and almost fell again. "I think you broke my damn knee," he said again, not moving.

"I'm not going to tell you again Breed...get over there," Tye said in a tone that Breed knew he was out of time so he took a deep breath and took a step...a very painful step...then another and another till he reached the travois, collapsing on it. Tye quickly tied his hands to the poles. He didn't tie his feet this time. It was still full dark when they moved out. Tye noticed the lightning was closer and the cool breeze that smelled of rain brought the rumble of the thunder with it. "We're going to get pretty wet partner," he said to Sandy patting him on the side of the neck.

185

Tye pulled his slicker out of the saddle bag and put it on, pulling the collar tight and his hat down low. They were not making good time pulling the travois because of detours to be made around huge clumps of cactus, small arroyos, and steep hills.

At the first dim light of dawn, the gray line of approaching rain could be seen behind them and moving fast. Lightning flashed and a never ending booming of thunder that was deafening had Sandy nervous as well as Tye. Lightning hit the rim of the canyon to his left about a quarter mile away. Tye immediately dismounted and looked for cover. He knew of men killed by lightning while sitting astride of their horse, and he had no desire to be another victim.

The rain, coming down in sheets, was falling as hard as Tye had ever seen.

"Dammit!" Breed said. "Get me under something before I drown."

"I'm looking Breed, but what's the difference...drown or hang. You are dead either way."

"I ain't hung yet, Watkins. It's still a ways to the fort and a lot can happen."

"You're right Breed. You may not make it to the fort." Breed started to say something else but thought better of it.. Tye continued walking, leading the skittish Sandy. Looking over his shoulder, he could see sunlight on the land behind him as the storm moved past them. In a couple minutes they were in the sunlight and the warm rays took the chill from the men. Steam rose from the two men and Sandy as they dried out.

Two hours later they hit the Old Mail Road and turned east toward Clark. An hour and a half later, Tye saw in the distance the buildings of Brackett and Fort Clark. He glanced down at Breed and saw he was still asleep. "He'll be surprised when he wakes up," Tye said out loud, a big grin on his face.

When he entered the outskirts of Brackett a man hollered that Tye was back and people came out of the hardware store and the saloons waving their hats and celebrating. No matter where you were in the west, men held men like Breed and his friends in disdain. A robber, a murderer, they could put up with but not with men who molested women and especially young girls like this man had. It would be a great day of celebration on the day he and the others were hung.

A few soldiers had gathered at the bridge over Los Moras Creek going into the fort. One of the soldiers came up to Tye and grabbed Sandy's reins.

"We'll take care of Sandy and that piece of dung you have behind him. Go see Rebecca."

Tye looked at the soldier. "Is she okay?"

187

"Sure she is. I just figured you needed to see her," the soldiers said, a big smile on his face.

"Thanks." Tye said dismounting. "Be sure Sandy gets some extra oats."

"Will do, Tye. Now get going."

Tye walked toward his house but stopped and turned to the soldier. "Tell Major Thurston I will see him in an hour or so." The soldier nodded.

Tye took a couple steps toward his home and then stopped, and turned back to the soldier. "Never mind telling the major anything. I'll go see him now." The soldier nodded again, and headed toward the stables with Sandy.

No use making the man wait. Besides, the first thing all soldiers do when coming in off patrol is report to the commanding officer and I don't want the men thinking I'm any different.

Major Thurston was standing on the porch waiting for him with a big smile on his face. "I see you brought Breed in... alive," he said as Tye stepped on the porch and shook the major's hand.

"Yes Sir, I did but only after some serious deliberation," Tye replied smiling.

"I never had a doubt you would if it was at all possible." Thurston said. "I know you pretty well and killing someone in cold blood no matter how much they deserve it is just not in you. You're just too good of man to do that."

Tye smiled as they both went into Thurston's office. Tye took a chair in front of the desk as Thurston sat in his behind the desk. "I really came close, Major. I wanted to kill him and do it in way that was as painful as possible."

Thurston laughed and leaned back in his chair. "From what I heard, you did a pretty good job of making him hurt some."

Tye nodded. "My pa told me one time if you ever want to put a man in some real hurt, kick him in the knee. I've done it before against some Apaches that I wasn't making any headway with in a fight. His falling backwards when I hit him and landing in some cactus wasn't planned, but it didn't hurt my feelings any either."

"I think the man deserved every damn thing he received," Thurston said with a grin that so big that Tye had to laugh also. Thurston leaned back again and asked, "Did you have any trouble in Mexico?"

"You mean with the Federales?" Thurston nodded. "No, never even saw any. Where I caught Breed was near a village that had a man whose father used to come to our home when I was a kid. He and pa were good friends. This man, his name is Pablo, helped me with Breed and I told him if he ever needed anything to let me know. So if someone named Pablo or a man says Pablo sent him to find me, please let me know." Thurston nodded.

"I understand the man killed and the two taken prisoner to Fort Inge were all relatives."

"Yes, Sir. Two of them were brothers and the youngest of the three was a nephew. The one killed by Breed was the oldest and the worst of the lot from what I can figure out. The brother taken to Inge was just a follower and the youngster never had a chance. He rode with his uncles and over time, became just like them."

"I've seen that before," Thurston said shaking his head. He stood up from his chair and Tye did also. They shook hands. "I guess that wraps up everything. We'll wait for the trial and until then unless something else comes up you can stay around here. Rebecca's not having any problems is she?"

"No Sir. She seems to be fine."

"Good. You take care of her and I'll see you when something comes up." Tye turned around and started to the door when Thurston said, "Good job, Tye...as usual." Tye smiled and continued out the door and toward his home.

Rebecca was waiting for him, along with Buff, on the porch. It does not take long for news to get around a fort, and they had already heard he was back. They hugged and kissed, and then the usual and expected remark came from Rebecca lips when

190

Tye came in from a patrol. She stepped back, pinched her nose and said, "Strip off those smelly clothes and your bath will be ready in a minute. You smell worse than a horse that has rolled in manure." She laughed and went inside to see if the water that was on the wood burning stove was hot enough. Tye sat down beside Buff on the porch.

"Did you report to the major?"

"That's what I like about the major," Tye said. "He gets to the point, finds out what he needs to know and then you are done." Tye looked at Buff.

"You've let her get a little bossy since I've been gone old man," Tye said, slapping Buff on the shoulder and laughing.

"Don't be calling me old you young pup. I just might have to teach you a lesson or two in the proper way to address your elders." They both laughed again and Tye stood up and stripped down to his breeches.

"I think I'll shave while she's getting the bath ready," the scout said. "By the way, after I clean up we need to get back to your telling me about pa.

Buff scratched the back of his neck. "I can't exactly remember where we stopped."

"You started talking about the winter of '26 that was the worse you had ever seen and ya'll found a cave to hole up in."

Buff nodded. "I remember. That was the coldest winter I had ever seen and never seen another like it. We'll talk after supper."

Chapter Nineteen

After bathing and eating a fine evening meal, Tye sat back in his chair and patted his stomach. "That was a fine meal honey...course after eating jerky and hard biscuits for a few days, anything would be good." He laughed heartily and slapped Buff on the shoulder.

"Well, you will be hard pressed to get another meal after that remark mister," Rebecca growled, standing with her arms folded across her breast, tapping her foot.

"Now, you know I was just funning you some," Tye said, knowing he had hurt her feelings. "You're the best cook in the world."

"Really!" She fired back, pretending to be upset. "You told me before that Mrs. O'Malley was the best in the world."

"Well...I...huh... that was before you started cooking for me."

"Sure," she said enjoying having him squirming some.

193

"Ain't she the best cook in the world, Buff?" Tye said, desperately looking for help from his friend.

Buff knew Rebecca was funning Tye. "Don't go bringing me in this because of your big mouth."

Tye was sure he was in trouble. "Honey, I…"

"Just hush before you make a bumbling fool of yourself in front of Buff," she said laughing. "We were just…as you would say, funning you."

"You're not mad then," Tye said standing up and hugging her.

"No, I'm not mad. It would take a lot more than that to ever make me mad at you." She kissed him and pulled away. "I've got dishes to wash so you and Buff continue your talk."

Buff lit his pipe, leaned back and shut his eyes. "You ever saw a blizzard, Tye?"

Tye shook his head. "No I haven't. I've seen it snow here a few times with a strong wind, but nothing like what pa had told me he had seen."

"A blizzard is something else. It might snow a foot in just a couple hours. With the wind, you may have a few inches of snow in one area where it is really blowing, and several feet deep in an area out of the wind. This particular one was a bad one. The storm lasted four days: four days of near zero temperatures, forty or so mile per hour winds, and three foot of snow. That summer at the rendezvous, we heard several trappers caught in areas they could not find good shelter had died...their bodies not found until the spring thaw. That was the storm that killed a friend of mine...George McIntosh."

Buff took several good puffs on his pipe before continuing. "Anyway Tye, we had been lucky to find this cave, otherwise you might have never been born. We probably would have died like so many others did in that storm. The storm was only the beginning. We had two months of temperatures so cold that your skin would freeze if exposed to the wind. Many of the Blackfoot and Ute's died those two months. Even a great number of elk, buffalo and other animals that were accustomed to harsh winters died."

"Anyway, the second day of the storm we knew we were in trouble. The horses had no grass and we were running out of firewood. Our food would last a couple more days, but we needed to find fresh meat before we ran out. In cold like this, a man's body needs more food than he normally would. The cave was on the side of a mountain and from the opening; it was a steep slope of maybe fifty or so feet to level ground. There was a sheet of ice under the snow making it dangerous to try and make your way down the slope. One slip and you could break a leg, or arm, or maybe something worse...like your fool neck. Getting the horses down was out of the question and they needed food now. A horse can do okay in snow, but if ice is under the snow it made things a little touchy. If a horse's hoof broke through the ice, the edges of the ice could cut his fetlocks. This could make it very uncomfortable for him to walk for awhile and if the horse slipped, he could easily break a leg. We knew we were in a fix." Buff hunched his shoulders and shuddered. "We were in enough trouble as it was, but you could double that if we lost any of our horses."

"There was a creek with grass along the edges and in the shallows about a half mile back where we come from and Ben was determined to go get some of that grass. The grass was brown, not green, and would not be real nutritional, but it would fill the horses' bellies.

The snow had let up some, but was still coming down in huge flakes. The wind had almost stopped. We knew with the huge flakes and no wind that the snow would be too deep to get through in twenty-four hours if it kept falling like this. The clouds were heavy and looked like they were not going away, so it was now or never."

Buff leaned back in his chair and puffed on his pipe as Rebecca came and sat down at the table with them. "We got some rope and tied one end to a rock just inside the cave's opening and threw the other end out of the cave down the slope. Ben could use this to hold onto and slide on his butt to level ground. Trying to walk down could turn into a painful experience with one slip."

"He made it down the slope with no problem. He left his Hawken in the cave carrying only his two pistols and butcher knife. No Indians would be out in this weather and the Grizzly was hibernating, so he figured having two hands free to carry grass was more important. He found the creek and gathered an armful of the damp grass and brought it back and placed it on the ground below the cave. Two more trips were made and he had a good pile ready to take up to the cave. Ben lashed the grass together with rawhide strips and tied the bundle to the rope which we hauled up to the cave. This was repeated three times. Ben hollered he was going to make a couple more trips. Jim hollered back that we had enough and to come on back up. Jim and I both knew how fast things could change and we had been watching the low clouds that were now coming in fast."

"Ben had already turned to leave and our words had fallen on nothing but the snow, ice, and snow heavy pines. Later, Ben said he thought he heard us holler something, but could not make it out and went on toward the creek.

"Later, Ben said he was almost back to the base of the mountain when the weather changed. When I say changed... I mean changed! Snow began to fall harder and the wind went from almost calm to thirty or forty miles per hour. It was whipping the snow from the ground into the air and mixing it with the new that was falling. A man could see only a few feet and we knew our friend was in trouble."

"In this situation, we knew better than to send one of us down the slope to help because then two men would be in trouble. We started hollering, hoping maybe he was close enough to hear our voices and follow the sound. He had traveled south from the cave and the wind was blowing from the north, so there was a good chance of him hearing us. He later told us what he went through, after which he said he hoped to never experience it again. He never heard our hollering at him. He said when the storm hit he was only one hundred yards or less away but with the snow being blown by the wind it was as if thousand tiny hail stones were hitting his face, stinging like hell. He could not see anything. He dropped the grass he had and it immediately was lifted into the air and disappeared with the wind. He took out one of his pistols and fired it into the air. We heard it and Jim fired his rifle, I fired mine, and then Stumpy fired his. We listened and head what sounded like another pistol shot so we all reloaded and fired again at ten second intervals. We waited and then the three of us all saw the rope tighten, and we knew Ben had found it and was coming up. When he was almost to the top, Stumpy reached and grabbed his hand and pulled him into the cave. He was near frozen so we stripped him naked, placed him near the fire and covered him with a buffalo robe. Jim got a cup of coffee and put the tin cup to Ben's lips so he could start warming him up from the inside out." Buff smiled again remembering Ben's reaction. "Old Ben's eyes flew open when the hot cup touched his lips, but he drank it. He tried to hold the cup, but he was shaking too much."

"About an hour later he was sitting up and telling us about his experience of near freezing to death. He said he thought of things like: why in hell he ever come to the Rockies, about his relatives that would probably never know what happened to him, and finally he said, he calmed down and accepted the fact he was going to die and was okay with it. He said he had said a little prayer and made his peace with God when he heard our first shot, then the second and third. He thought he had the direction they come from and moved quickly, at least as fast as a man half froze to death could move, toward the sound. The second round of shots sounded almost like they were above him and that was when he found the rope."

"Ben was okay and the horses were happy with the grass, but we still had a problem: little firewood and short on food and the storm showed no sign of letting up. We had enough wood for the night and maybe tomorrow, but after that it was going to be a cold cave. We cut back on the size of the fire to preserve wood. We bedded down as close as we could to the fire. One of us would stay awake at all times to make sure the fire did not go out. Dark settled in and the wind howling outside of our cave was so loud it was hard to go to sleep. Stumpy took the first watch and I was to take the second and Bridger the last. Ben was going to get a lot sleep and get his strength back."

"During Jim's watch, Stumpy, Ben, and me all woke up at the same time. We saw Jim standing at the mouth of the cave looking out. We all realized why we woke up at the same time…it was quiet. The wind had died down and besides the crackling of the wood in our fire, there was no sound. The storm had passed and the calm that always follows had arrived."

"The cold dawn came with a sky heavy with low, dark grey clouds that held the promise of more snow to come. For now though, the wind had stopped and we had a little time to do things like find food and gather firewood. We had not discussed it but each of us thought this was a good place to ride out the winter. We took our tomahawks and cut steps in the ice leading down from the cave. I left to get more grass for the horses, Stumpy and Ben gathered firewood and Bridger went hunting. By noon we had plenty of grass and enough firewood for at least a week. We were exhausted from going up and down the slope, not only from climbing, but the strain we put on ourselves of being afraid of slipping and being seriously injured. About mid afternoon we heard a shout and we all scrambled to the cave opening. Jim was hollering to throw down the rope so he could tie on the hind quarters of a deer he had shot. Stumpy went down and they tied the meat on and we hauled it up. The two of them left to get the rest and were back just before the sun dropped behind the mountain. Jim made the comment that game was the scarcest he had ever seen."

"It had been a small buck that Jim had shot and we had maybe sixty or seventy pounds of meat. We cut the meat into steaks and strips for cooking. With the cold there was no problem with meat spoiling in the Rockies. The horses were fine, we had food for a few days if we ate sparingly, plenty of firewood, and things were looking up. We bedded down that night with full bellies and a cozy fire. The next few days would be spent molding bullets, repairing saddles, bridles, and traps. As a matter of fact, the whole winter was spent by trappers doing nothing but this. It's a time my friend Joe Meek described as 'busy idleness."

"There were a few more storms, but we made sure we had plenty of grass, wood, and food at all times by going out when the weather allowed. Despite the severity of the winter, we were comfortable. Like I said earlier, we were very fortunate to find this cave."

Rebecca, who had sat down earlier after washing and putting up the dishes, had a question. "Buff, before you continue your stories about Ben I've always wondered about a few things about you trappers. Listening to stories from my father that he had heard, I wondered who made your clothes and did you have a balanced diet with meat and vegetables, and were a lot of you married?"

Buff howled and slapped his knee. "We had a balanced diet...meat, meat, and more meat, with some berries thrown in every once in awhile. You would not have liked what we ate, Rebecca. Most civilized people wouldn't. We lived like the Indians. When we had plenty of meat, we gorged ourselves. Buffalo was the best meat followed by venison and other animals. The best was hump ribs from the buffalo which when cooked over buffalo chips had a peppery flavor. The liver was usually eaten raw. During starving times a trapper might eat his own moccasins, a dog, or the ears off his mule. A man would be surprised what he would eat if he is hungry enough. Warm buffalo blood reminded most of us of milk." He stopped as Rebecca gagged and put her hand to her mouth.

"I'm sorry I asked," she said forcing a smile.

"It wasn't an easy life, Rebecca. Despite what people read in the dime novels, it was not a glorious life. Death could come in a lot of ways and it could come quick and unexpected. As far as wives, many of the trappers had them...Indian wives which they had bought from the girls father with horses, guns, furs, or any number of things. Most did not stay with the women long, but some stayed together for years and raised families. A trapper who did not have a woman made his own clothes. We had a possible bag which we carried that had things like needles and thread, flint and steel for starting fires. Our clothes were skins of animals like the deer and beaver. A heavy buffalo robe would keep a man reasonably warm in the coldest weather. Every once in a while, we would splurge at the rendezvous and buy clothes like wool shirts and pants, but they didn't last long. It was a tough existence for the trapper, but if you wanted a life of seeing things no white man had seen before, doing what you wanted to do, and answering to no man…it was all worth while."

Rebecca stood up satisfied she had her answers. "I think I'll leave you men here to talk. I'm a little tired and going to bed." She walked around the table and hugged Tye and gave him a kiss and then gave Buff a peck on the cheek. "Goodnight," she said and received the same from both men.

"I don't think she thinks too much of a trappers way of life," Tye said laughing. Buff smiled, closed his eyes and leaned back in his chair thinking of buffalo hump and beaver tail. Tye interrupted his thoughts with a question. "Did anything happen in the spring?"

Buff downed the rest of the whiskey in his glass. "The spring was the real start of the trouble with the Blackfoot and the

Ute's. Those devils began making a real effort to rid the mountains of us trappers. Before, they roamed in small groups, but now they were uniting and raising hell. Trapping alone was just asking to be killed."

Buff picked up his empty glass and looked at Tye. "Okay you old coot." Tye got up and walked to the cabinet and came back with a bottle and filled Buff's glass as well as his own. "Go on," Tye said.

"The snow had not disappeared when we heard about the trouble. A group of trappers wanting to get an early start like we did came into our camp that we had set up along Bear Creek. They said George Shaffer, Bill Lang, and two other trappers they did not know had been killed. George and Bill were friends of mine and top notch trappers and the fact they had been killed surprised me. Every year men were killed, but most of the time there were green trappers with little experience. Your experienced men didn't take unnecessary chances and they recognized a dangerous situation before they walked into it. The fact that George and Bill were killed really bothered me."

"The visitors stayed the night in our camp, and we talked long into the night about the Indian situation. The conclusion was that it was going to be a dangerous season and the five men that came into our camp, at Jim's invitation, decided to stay with us and work their traps. That gave us nine men and assuming they were good shots and fighters, would give us a good chance even against a large party of Blackfoot. I was the oldest and most experienced of the bunch and of course they had heard of Jim's and Stumpy's exploits. They sure as hell heard of your pa's killing the four Blackfoot in hand to hand battle and also the fight with the grizzly. Considering all this they were glad to be with us and would follow our suggestions. We decided not to spread ourselves to far apart in running our traps so if trouble came we could help each other. We would work in pairs with one setting his traps while the other kept an eye for trouble, and then the two would move up the creek so the other could set his traps."

"We did this for two weeks with no problems and we were trapping a lot of beaver. I worked with Ben, Jim with Absher, Wolf with LaCroix, and Shipley and Longley were a team. Since there were nine of us, we would alternate with one of us staying in camp watching the horses and supplies. The first was Grissom. We worked about two miles of the creek at a time both ways from camp...a mile up river and a mile down river. Under normal circumstances the last trap may be two miles or more from camp. We hiked to and from our traps leading a pack horse, but being a lot closer than normal to camp, if a shot was fired, help could come in a few short minutes. We set our traps twice a day...early and late. During mid day we would flesh the plews from the beaver we had caught that morning. After fleshing, which is scraping the fat and meat off the plews, we would stretch them on hoops made of green willow branches and allow them to dry. After curing, we would roll them tightly and pack them away. Like I said a minute ago, we all were doing well. Things changed the next morning."

Chapter Twenty

"This particular morning, Ben and I were the closest to camp with Jim and Stumpy the furthest which was maybe a mile and a half up stream with Wolf and LaCroix in between. Shipley and Grissom were down stream maybe a quarter mile with Langley taking his turn watching camp. I was taking a beaver out of my trap when we heard the shot which came from the direction of camp. Ben and I dropped everything, grabbed our Hawken's, and started running in the direction of camp, keeping our eyes moving, looking for trouble as we ran. The first shot was a rifle and the second shot was a pistol. Ben was ahead of me because he could run like a damn deer. I saw him pull up and take aim, and then saw the smoke from the rifle before I heard it. I was beside him by then and took aim at a Blackfoot and fired. I guess I was breathing to hard or something because I missed. There were six of them and they were all over Langley fixing to kill him when Ben fired killing one and then I fired. They looked in our direction and quickly ran the other way. We went directly to where Langley was and saw he was hurt pretty bad. I kneeled down beside him and saw he was in obvious pain. They had shot him in the shoulder with an arrow and were in the process of holding him down and scalping him alive when we showed up. They had not completed the cuts to jerk the scalp away from the skull. He would live but Bridger was going to have some stitching to do to put the scalp back in place. He was good at doctoring."

"A minute later, Wolf and LaCroix showed up a running as fast as they could and were followed by Shipley and Grissom. All were hollering, wanting to know what happened. It got real quiet in a hurry when they saw Langley. They stood over their friend with genuine concern showing on their faces. I was kneeling beside Langley and looked up at LaCroix, his eyes fixed on mine. "He gonna be alright," he asked?

I nodded. "He's going to live alright but he's going to be done for awhile. Bridger is good at stitching so he'll fix his scalp but he's going to have some scars. First thing we need to do is get that shaft out of his shoulder. I was afraid those red devils might just come back with some friends so I told Wolf and Grissom to stand watch. LaCroix and Ben would help me with Langley."

"We sat him up. Ben was behind him holding his shoulders. I took my butcher knife and cut the shaft to about three inches from his shoulder. The tip had not broke the skin in the back of his shoulder but there was a bulge where the point was pushing the skin out. LaCroix took his knife from the fire where he had placed it to sterilize the blade. He cut the skin where it appeared the point was. I placed a bottle of whiskey I had taken from my saddle bags and placed it in Langley's right hand. I told him to take a stiff drink as I picked up a flat rock. When he tilted his head back to take a swig I hit the shaft with the flat rock and the flint point broke through the cut LaCroix had made and protruded three inches from his back. LaCroix grabbed the shaft and jerked the bloody thing the rest of the way out. This all took less than three seconds and was over before the pain registered on Langley's brain."

Buff laughed and downed some whiskey. He looked at Tye. "Do you need to get in there with Rebecca?"

"She's fine Buff...probably asleep by now. Now go on with the story."

"Okay...okay. Hell I haven't talked this much at one time in my whole sorry life.

"Well, we got that shaft out before he knew what was happening, but the next two steps he wouldn't be so lucky. He screamed bloody hell when I poured whiskey in the hole in his shoulder and the hole in his back. It was bleeding pretty good which was good. He calmed down and I told him to drink some more of the whiskey. His eyes grew wide when he saw the blade with the tip that was glowing red. He knew what was coming and nodded for me to get it over with. LaCroix handed him a piece of leather and he chomped down on it. His face was red and his cheeks were puffed out when I melted the skin over the holes with the hot blade. The stench of burnt flesh made you wrinkle your nose, but it was done. Langley was fixed up except for his scalp and I told him Bridger should be along shortly. He was drunk by now and his words were a little slurred. Yu tal ole Bridger tha I had bett'r be as gud luking when he's thru as I wus this mornin'. He then passed out which was a blessing because it was going to take a while to stitch his scalp back on and it would not be pleasant for him if he was awake."

"About that time, Wolf hollered Bridger and Stumpy was coming in. I filled the two in what had happened and Jim began to stitch Langley's scalp back on. He worked about thirty minutes before he was through and everyone was impressed with the job. I think if Jim had stayed a civilized man he would have been one of them doctors that operate on people."

Langley was still out when Jim called us all in around the fire. It was mid afternoon with about three hours of daylight left. Jim told us what we all knew already. Those Blackfoot would be back with their friends and with Langley hurt, we could not run. We had to fort up. We moved our camp to the edge of the creek. There was heavy brush along the bank and the stream was deep so we figured our backside would be safe. Ben and Wolf used Ben's horse to pull some logs to the bank where we stacked them to where we could stand and see over the top one. Our position was a good one. We had water just a couple steps away, we had food, we had plenty of powder and lead, and counting Langley's weapons we had seven Kentucky long rifles plus mine and Ben's Hawken's. We had nine single shot pistols, and we each had a knife and tomahawk. We had a clear field of fire for maybe fifty yards. They might get us if they came, but they were going to pay a heavy price."

"We settled in for what we figured would be a long siege…if we survived the first attack. We hauled and stacked some firewood. We pulled and stacked grass for the horses which were picketed in the brush just to our left and below the bank, so they were pretty well protected. We felt we could not have picked a better spot to defend if we had looked for a year. We stretched out to get some shut eye before what we figured would be a long night. We had one man awake now and after dark we would have two awake at all times. With our horses and pack animals only a few feet away they would serve as a third set of eyes and ears. There is no better sentry than a horse and we had nine or ten of them plus the mules." Buff chuckled and added. "Course the mules were not sentries like the horses, but if a

211

damn Blackfoot Injun got among them they would bite and kick the hell out of them. There's nothing meaner or more ornery than a mule when he wants to be. The only thing against us was the moon not being a full moon. It was going to be pretty damn dark."

We had just settled when we heard the unmistakable booms of three or four long rifles followed by pistol shots. They came from our left which was down river. We grabbed our guns and peered over the logs we had stacked up just in time to see four trappers riding like hell. They were going to pass about forty yards in front of us. Hot on the heels of their horses were twenty or twenty five screaming Blackfoot warriors.

Chapter Twenty One

"No self respecting trapper was going to let a fellow trapper get killed by or worse, be captured by the Blackfoot if he could help it, so we cut loose with our long rifles at them devils. Like I said earlier, most trappers were better than average when it came to shooting and our fifty caliber balls caught them by surprise. Four were blown from their pony's backs and another went head over heels when his pony collapsed. He hit the ground hard and didn't move." Shakespeare laughed before he continued. All of us fired and we knocked four Injuns off their ponies and one pony went down. Everyone hit what they aimed at they said and no one would admit to missing...but some did."

"The remaining Blackfoot veered off and rode away not knowing how many enemies had shot at them. The trappers slowed and turned back toward us, and waving, came toward our little fort. Jim and I looked at each and grinned when we saw who they were. Three of the four were the men who had jumped Ben at the rendezvous when he had whipped the hell out of the biggest of the three. We glanced over at your pa and we both

213

knew from the look on his face he recognized them. The men dismounted and after thanking us, the big man, who obliviously recognized Ben, walked over to him. In the best way he could, he told Ben he was sorry about the fight and stuck out his hand. Ben hesitated a moment and looked at me. I nodded, and he took the man's hand. The man told everyone that this here young whippersnapper had licked him fair and square and it was over as far as he was concerned. There was no reason for the three to recognize us because we had cold-cocked the other two from behind with our rifles."

"We got a problem Jim told us. It was obvious that those Blackfoot was not the ones that attacked earlier or they would have known we were here. That means we now have two groups of the devils that know where we are. He told the men to put their horses with ours and step behind the logs with us. Four more guns could only help. Our little party now was twelve healthy men and one wounded...twelve men that were good shots would be a formidable task for the Blackfoot that was for sure."

"Darkness settled around us quickly, as it always does in the Rockies when the sun drops behind the mountains. We sat around the small fire discussing plans to defend ourselves if the attack came. I said if, but we all knew it was coming and we figured at first light. It was Ben who came up with the idea of how we could handle things. He suggested we all fire our long guns when the attack came. After we all fired six would drop behind the logs and begin reloading the rifles while the other five fired their pistols plus the pistols of the men reloading the guns. This would give a total of twenty-four or so rounds counting the guns of the wounded Langley. Twenty-four rounds in a short span of time from men who were good shots could have a devastating affect on the Injuns. In the seconds it took to fire the two rounds from the pistols the rifles should be reloaded and ready to fire again and the men behind the logs would begin reloading the pistols." Tye interrupted Buff.

"I saw pa's old Hawken and even shot it a few times. How fast could a man reload one? It looked to be a job by the time one put the powder down the barrel, used the rod to compact the wadding on top of the powder, drop the ball in and ram it down the barrel, then replace the rod.

"The average time to load one was probably twenty to twenty-five seconds but an experience hunter could fire and reload four times a minute. Maybe three if he was being shot at by a bunch of screaming Injuns," he added laughing. "Anyway, Ben, me, Jim, Stumpy and the Frenchman, LaCroix would be the five shooters. We laid out fifty caliber lead balls, powder and wadding so they would be easily accessible all along the wall. We took the rods out of the rifles and placed them by the lead,

215

powder, and wadding. It would save a few seconds by not having to pull them out and replace them in the holder under the barrel of the guns. The short rods of the pistols were laid out also. We set the guard schedule and lay down to get some shut eye, but as you know, it's damn hard to go to sleep when you know a fight is coming at first light. It was going to be a long night."

"Along about midnight the horses began to act up...ears twitching, snorting, and all staring into the blackness in front of us. Horses could see and hear better than a man, especially at night. They saw or heard something that we could not, and believe me; it made each of us nervous as hell. The devils could be sneaking up and be almost on top of us in the dark for all we knew."

"We all were straining our eyes and ears, looking, listening...but there was no movement or sound. The horses had settled down and the only sound one could hear was his own heart beating. Finally, I said it must have been a panther or some other varmint that had disturbed the horses. We all lay back down except for the two on sentry. Like I said earlier, at times like this no one was sleeping...just staring at the dark sky. When you know you are going into a fight where a lot of men are going to die, a man has all kinds of thoughts go through his head: if you had family, you wondered if you would see them again or if you told them you loved them the last time you saw them. Another thing was second guessing the decision you had made to become a trapper that put you in this situation in the first place. Finally, most of us made peace with God and once again made promises of what we would do or not do if He would just help us out of this situation. For myself, having no family, I was doing I wanted to do, made peace with God and spent a long time staring at the beautiful snow capped mountains whose white tops were visible in the dark. In the end though, you would decide that you were doing what you wanted to do and this was just another situation that you knew would come up if you stayed out here long enough. Just accept the situation, and do your best to help your friends and yourself stay alive."

"Ben and I had the last watch. It was with the first dim light of dawn that we saw them. There were close to seventy-five of them sitting on their ponies across the meadow, maybe two hundred yards away. One began riding back and forth in front of the rest screaming, obliviously trying to whip the rest into a killing frenzy, which didn't take much with a Blackfoot warrior."

"The others with us were up immediately when the first warrior began his hollering, and in a few seconds you never heard such a racket as all of them devils were screaming and whipping their ponies back and forth. Twelve long rifles lay across the logs, hammer's back, fingers on the triggers. It was cool that morning but there were twelve men sweating like it was midday in July. Ben I think was the coolest of us. Like I told you before, he would go crazy when he was preparing to go into a fight." Buff began chuckling and when Tye asked him what was funny he said. "Your pa jumped over the log fort and started screaming and doing some sort of stupid war dance. The Blackfoot stopped and watched. I would have given anything to know what they were thinking or saying while watching this crazy white man. They knew who it was though, you can bet your life on that. Your pa was big medicine to them and greatly respected as a warrior. Besides, not too many trappers were anywhere as close to being as big as he was so it wasn't hard to pick him out of a crowd."

"As nervous as we were, there wasn't a one of us that was not smiling at the sight of Ben hollering and doing that dance. The smiles faded when we heard the hooves of the ponies pounding the ground and followed by the war cries of the warriors as they charged. Ben vaulted back over the wall and told everyone to hold their fire until they were at seventy yards. There was not a one of us who had not fought the Blackfoot before, so even as nervous as we were, everyone held their fire. When Ben fired, his shot was followed by eleven fifty caliber long rifles booming as one making a tremendous noise. Eight or nine warriors somersaulted over the rears of their ponies and one horse went down, throwing its rider. Six men dropped behind the walls and quickly begin reloading the long guns. Six pistols roared and this time four warriors fell from their ponies. At forty yards, six more guns poured lead and four more Indians fell from their ponies and one slumped over his pony's neck, barely holding on to the horse's mane. The rest veered away and headed back across the meadow. The long rifles were reloaded and we aimed again and fired as they rode away. Two more were knocked from the back of their ponies at a distance of nearly eighty yards which was good shooting considering the distance and moving targets."

"We were relieved we had survived the attack without injury to anyone but we knew this was just the beginning. The smoke from the rifles hung thick in the early morning air. Through the smoke, we could see fifteen or twenty warriors lying in the short grass of the meadow in front of us. We took turns going to the creek to drink water. It's funny how dry your throat quickly becomes during a battle."

"Culhane, he's the man that Tye had whipped at the rendezvous, congratulated Tye on his plan. The others that came in with Culhane were Simpson, Perkins, and Gentry and they did the same and again thanked all of us for helping them out. Jim said that we might not have survived the attack if they had not been here, so I guess we were all square with each other. The Blackfoot were again about two hundred yards away and were apparently in a heated discussion on how to get to us. Ben got himself a piece of Buffalo hump and his canteen. He said he would stand watch. The rest of us sat down behind the log wall and chewed on some hump ourselves...and waited for the next attack. We didn't have to wait long.

"Ben hollered they were getting ready to come again. Everyone was up immediately and at the wall. We had decided to use the same plan as before. The Blackfoot were whipping themselves into a frenzy again hollering and running their ponies back and forth. Ben, who had eyes as good as an eagle, said they had several warriors on the ground with bows. As he spoke, the ones on the ground fired their arrows high into the air. We all followed the flight with our eyes and knew they were going to fall a little short. They fell about forty yards short of our wall. As we watched, they moved closer and released more arrows into the sky. We watched again and knew this time they were going to be close. We ducked behind the wall as arrows thudded into the logs and into the brush behind us."

"We knew their plan now. An Injun could fire several arrows a minute. They would keep arrows coming in to keep our heads down while they attacked. This was going to get bloody and not all of it Blackfoot blood. Bridger said the only chance we have is to ignore the arrows and keep shooting or they would over run us. That was going to be hard to do, but we knew it was true. It was choice of maybe an arrow hitting you, or a sure bet to get a knife in you or a bashed in head from a tomahawk when the 'Red Sticks' over run us. We would stand and fire and take our chances with the arrows."

"We fired our rifles again and those heavy lead balls did some damage as several warriors left their pony's backs. Arrows thudded into the logs and the softer thump of one hitting flesh was followed by a curse. Culhane was down and Grissom took his place. At forty yards we fired the pistols and at least three maybe four more Injuns hit the ground hard. Another wave of arrows came in and Ben took one in the left shoulder and Absher had one glance off his skull and he was down. Wolf and Simpson came up from reloading and stood at the wall just as we fired the pistols again, including Ben who fired despite the arrow in his shoulder. I know some more of them went down but we didn't have time to look as the rifles were handed back to us."

They were on top of us and we fired from the hip and then threw the guns down and grabbed our knives or hatchets. Rather than be confined in the area behind the logs, we all leaped over the wall to face them in hand to hand fighting in open ground.

Another wave of arrows came in and they helped us as several of the devils took arrows from behind from their own archers."

Ben was the first over the wall and stood there screaming and slashing with his knife, and despite the arrow, swinging the hatchet with his left. He had two down before any of us had taken a swing. I saw Bridger go down with a brave on him but I couldn't help...I had one in the air coming at me after leaping from his pony's back. I swung my hatchet and caught him in the side of the head. The hatchet went in deep and it was wrenched from my hand as the Indian fell limply at my feet with my hatchet firmly stuck in the side of his head. I pulled my Green River Knife and faced another. He took a swing at my belly and while doing so, his foot slipped and he went down. I was on him quick and planted that Green River Knife plum to the hilt in his chest. The fight lasted maybe a minute...minute and a half at most, and it was over. The Blackfoot, at least those that could, joined the bowman and left."

"I could not believe it nor could the others...those still standing anyway. We looked around and it was a sight I would never forget. Everywhere you looked were bodies of dead or wounded men...both red and white. That was the time that I first saw a side of your pa that I would see again and again. He never killed a man for no reason. There were two Blackfoot warriors hurt pretty badly. You pa gave them some water, helped them up and got them started walking away from us. They kept looking over their shoulder expecting a bullet in the back. They knew who he was and this act we knew would only make him bigger medicine in their way of thinking.

We hurt them pretty bad but we were hit hard too. Wolf was dead, a knife in his chest and his head bashed in by a tomahawk. Langley, who had been injured earlier, had taken an arrow in the chest as he lay behind the wall and was dead. Simpson was dead with a split skull. Stumpy was still woozy from the arrow that glanced off his skull, Culhane had an arrow in his shoulder as did Ben. Bridger came out of the fight with the Indian I saw take him down and only had a cut on his hand."

"The area where your pa was had five Blackfoot scattered around with either split skulls or bellies ripped open. He was a fighting man like none of us had ever seen...completely fearless. We stacked the dead Blackfoot and counted them...forty-one. They hurt us but we gave them something to think about the next time they cornered some trappers. As bad as we hurt them we knew when they left they would not be back...not today anyway. We also knew we had to move and move quickly."

"We tied our dead on their horses and left, headed up stream away from the direction the Indians had gone. We traveled maybe six miles before we stopped to make camp with about an hour of daylight left. It was full dark by the time we had buried our friends and took care of the wounds of Ben and Culhane. Absher was fine other than a headache and Bridger had sewed up the cut on his left hand himself. We collapsed in our bedrolls exhausted, but damn glad to be alive."

Chapter Twenty Two

"We all stayed together until it was time to go to the rendezvous. We figured it would be safer if we did, even though it cut down on the number of plews each had. We had no more trouble that year but at the rendezvous we found out plenty others had. This year's get together was to be held at Cache Valley, and when we arrived, it didn't take long to find out the main topic of discussion...the Blackfoot and Ute. It was estimated that maybe fifty trappers had died at their hands this spring. There were some new faces at the rendezvous but there were a lot of faces we would know that were not...some were friends and others just a name you recognized. The bodies of some had been found and buried; others were never found or heard from again.

"I had only three hundred and twenty pelts. Ben had a few more and Jim and Absher about the same as me. After buying supplies I had a little less than two hundred dollars left. Outside of card games there was no place to spend the money so that was okay. I still had money left from the year before so I had a little

225

nest egg started. Ben did the best that year. If I remember correctly he had almost three hundred after supplies. I know he said it was the most money he had ever had at one time in his life."

"The rendezvous lasted two weeks...fourteen days of drinking, games, bragging, and remembering friends that were not there." Buff smiled. "A hell of lot of whiskey was drunk in their memory. Culhane made it known to all about our fight and especially about Ben's war dance and killing Blackfoot with a knife and hatchet. The story, which was stretched just a mite, added to Ben's respect among his fellow trappers. Culhane had Ben killing a total of twenty warriors and overall we killed almost a hundred. He only increased the total by about three times."

"Like we did at the first rendezvous, the trappers attending decided before we left that the next rendezvous would be held at Bear Lake. This was good news to our group because that would be close to where we would be trapping."

"After the rendezvous we headed back to Bear Creek, almost a week away. Ben's and Culhane's wounds had healed completely but even though Ben was not at full strength, no one had challenged him to any fights during the two week camp. He had been trapping only a little over a year and had achieved the respect of the trappers on par with Meek, Fitzgerald, and Bridger."

"I'll tell you straight, Tye. Over the years Ben would over shadow them but due to his not wanting to brag or even talk about things he did, he did not receive the attention of the rest of the country. He didn't talk much to the newspaper men or writers for the dime novels that begin showing up at the rendezvous every year. He would leave the talking to men like Bridger who could talk forever on any subject, especially his own self. I'm not taking anything away from Jim, he was my friend, and he was one hell of a trapper, but he liked to talk, and that's why you and everyone else read more about him than other men like your pa. But I tell you Tye, no trapper had more respect of the other trappers that you pa did and that's a fact." Buff stood up and stretched. "It's getting late. How about we hit the bed and continue this tomorrow?"

Tye stood up and shook Buff's hand. "We'll do that. Thanks for telling me about Ben, Buff. I've always been curious about his life."

"There's more to tell, Tye," Buff said nodding his head. "There's a lot more to tell. I'll see you in the morning." Buff walked to his room and shut the door.

Not yet sleepy, Tye opened the door and stepped out on the porch and sat down on the top step. The night air was crisp and smelled fresh, like it does after a rain. He leaned back, elbows on the porch, and looked up at the dark night sky with its ten thousand twinkling stars. He picked out the Big Dipper, the North Star, and several constellations that his pa had pointed out to him years ago. He thought of Ben and all the lessons he had taught him from the time he could walk until the day he was killed. Everything he was today was because of the things Ben had taught him. He promised himself he would do the same for his son…if it was a son. If the baby was a girl, that would be okay. She would be the best tracking, best shot, best fighting woman in the country. He smiled at that and thought, no; if the baby was a girl she would be a lady, just like her mother. He stood up, looked at the stars one more time, walked across the porch and back into the house to go to bed. He was anxious for the morning to come so he could hear more about Buff's and his father's adventures in the Rockies.

The morning dawned bright and clear. After breakfast, Rebecca went to see Mrs. O'Malley, leaving Tye and Buff alone to continue Buff's stories. It was Saturday and with no drilling of new recruits Sergeants Christian and Arnold dropped by just as Tye and Buff sat down on the porch. After shaking hands, Tye told his friends some of what Buff had told him and that they were just fixing to continue and they were welcome to sit in.

Buff lit his pipe and began talking. "We reached Bear Creek eight days after the rendezvous. Culhane stayed with us but Perkins and Gentry went their own way. The fall trapping was good along the creek and we all had around one hundred-seventy or so plews. This was not counting the mink, fox, and other varmints we had trapped and skinned which we could sell or make clothing from.

"We had no problem with the Ute or the Blackfoot and as winter settled in we made our way back to the cave. We camped there again this winter and a couple more times in years to come. We were pretty comfy there no matter what the weather was outside. There was seldom any Indian trouble during the winter months in the Rockies. The Indians and the trappers were like the grizzly...hibernating so to speak."

The winter was nothing compared to the previous one. There was the usual several feet of snow but no long periods of sub zero weather like the year before. We had days that the temperature reached the high twenties. When there was a break in the weather we gathered firewood and would shoot an elk or mountain buffalo. Mostly, we just sat around mending clothes, repairing traps, and molding bullets, waiting for the spring trapping season to arrive."

Gary McMillan

Chapter Twenty Three

"The warm weather came and the snow was beginning to melt from the low lands.   In the highlands, the snow never completely went away in the highest elevations. Man wasn't the only creature glad to see the winter end. The birds were flying, and deer and elk were frolicking all over the place. Wolves and panthers, thin from the long winter, were on the prowl. But best of all, beaver were on the banks chewing down the trees and taking the limbs to build new dams or repairing the old ones. Everywhere one looked; there was one of God's creatures running around happy the cold was gone."

"Of course there was one drawback: the Ute and Blackfoot were about also and one better not forget to be alert for them. They had a way of surprising a man and it was usually a fatal surprise.   With Culhane with us, along with LaCroix and Grissom, we numbered seven men. Seven was not a large party but we knew what we were doing and was not going to get ambushed. We kept the weapons of our friends that were killed so our little group was well armed.   If we were attacked, the

231

Blackfoot or Ute's could expect close to thirty accurate shots fired at them pretty damn quick. We decided we would do the same this year as before for protection: six would pair up and trap together while the odd man out watched the camp. We would swap out every three days and all would end up watching the camp over a three week period. We all would get equal time trapping this way and be a little safer than trapping alone."

"Hungry wolves roaming in packs were always a danger as well as the panther, and the Indians. The one thing we feared most though was old Ephraim. This time of the year he came out of hibernation hungry and in a foul mood. A man just didn't want to mess with one under no circumstances. The first morning of setting traps Jim and I came across the tracks of a huge grizzly on the banks of Bear Creek, right where we were going to set some traps. This was big bear, probably close to seven or eight hundred pounds and from the looks of the tracks; it was not a first time visit to this particular spot on the bank by the bear. We figured he would be back so being the brave souls we were," Buff chuckled some, "We decided to move on farther up the creek even though it put us farther from camp than we liked. Ben had drawn the short stick so he was in camp first. LaCroix and Grissom were teamed up as well as Absher and Culhane. We were up stream from camp and the other four were trapping down stream."

"The sun set on that first day and we settled in preparing for a long night. It would be long because no one slept a lot on the first night because of the anticipation of the next day. After the first day or so, a man was so damn tired he was glad to hit his bedroll and had no trouble sleeping."

"I remember that first morning like it was yesterday. After a night of thinking of all the beaver we were going to trap the sun breaking over the mountains brought us a sight we were not expecting. A large group of trappers sat on their horses facing our camp. I recognized a couple of them and knew they were voyageur's, which were trappers that worked for one of the fur companies. They were mostly French Canadian. We were 'free trappers' and worked for ourselves and answered to no one.

A man approached the camp and we figured him to be the Chef De Voyage or leader of the party. He spoke in French which we all could understand some but not enough to carry on a decent conversation. LaCroix walked forward and in French asked the man what he wanted. They talked for a few minutes and then left. LaCroix said they were recruiting trappers to work for the Hudson Bay Fur Company. I told him we were not interested...we were 'free trappers'. I told him Jim Bridger was our 'booshway.' Booshway was the term given to the leader of a group of trappers. I saw him look our way during the conversation. LaCroix told him I was there as well as Absher

233

and Ben. He asked Lacoix about the story of all the 'red sticks' Ben supposedly killed. Red sticks were a term us trappers used for Indians. LaCroix told him the story was true. He was impressed by our group and seemed peaceable enough, but LaCroix recognized three men with him that he had heard rumored had killed and robbed trappers. No one ever proved it though. Just the same, we figured we had better watch for any trappers in the area."

"We waited about an hour after the men left before we headed out to run and bait our traps. We were waiting to see if they came back. There had been some killings between the 'free trappers' and the trappers who worked for the fur companies. Bridger had tried the company way once and it wasn't worth the effort. The fur companies made all the money while the trapper did all the work. Ben stayed in camp to watch things when we left."

Buff stopped talking, emptied and refilled the bowl of his pipe. After lighting it and inhaling, he continued. "Ben had asked Jim and me about the thieving trappers while we waited to see if they come back or not. Jim said if we caught them we would shoot them. Well, this took old Ben back some. He said something like, you just can't shoot them. You can't take the law in your hands. Jim got a little upset and asked Ben what law he was talking about. The nearest law was two or three hundred miles away. Up here we have trapper's law and that law is, if you steal from another trapper…you are going to die. I told Ben that every instance I had heard about when the thieves were caught they put up a fight. It's not like we just line them up and shoot them. They have to be stopped because sooner or later, they may kill honest trappers. He understood that when it was put to him that way. Like I said earlier, Ben had a knack for being fair and I just hoped that idea would not get him killed some day. Anyway, that first day was great. All our traps had beaver in them and old Ben; well he was fit to be tied for not getting to set his. He knew the rules we agreed on and would wait, but I know he was frustrated as hell."

"The morning of the fourth day was liberation day for Ben. LaCroix was in camp and Ben was teamed with Grissom. Ben ran LaCroix's traps taking three Beaver. He took up the Frenchmen's traps and set his. After running Grissom's traps and taking three from them also, they headed back to camp about mid morning with the beavers and LaCroix's traps. They had a load with six beaver that weighed about thirty or so pounds each, and six traps that weighed five pounds each. They struggled with the load to where they had picketed the mule and placed their load on him. They were in great spirits as they headed back to camp a mile or so away."

We stayed in this spot for a week before moving up stream another four miles. That last day we only had seven beaver among us even though most of our traps had been sprung. No one said anything but I know I wondered about that. I think the others did also.

At the new camp it would be Jim's time to hold down the camp. Ben teamed with me, Absher with LaCroix and Grissom with Culhane. We set up camp before leaving to set our traps and arrived back just at dark. Sitting in the dark on our bedrolls Culhane brought the subject up: he asked if he was the only one that was suspicious about the empty traps. We all looked at each other before Jim spoke up. He said that he felt we all had our suspicions' but we would wait to see if it happened again. He asked if anyone saw any tracks around that were not ours. We hadn't. A man had their own way of walking and own footprints. An experience tracker could tell one man's tracks from another mans just as he could tell one horses tracks from another horse. We went to sleep that night with the thought that we were facing some thieves and we had a pretty good idea who they were. The strange part was the lack of tracks."

"The next morning Ben and I was running our traps. Ben was livid over the fact he had two beaver and three sprung traps. I had two also and two sprung traps. Like I said Ben was more than upset." Buff looked at Tye. "I guess you know about Ben's temper?"

Tye nodded his head and Sergeant Arnold spoke up. "So that's where your temper comes from, huh Tye?"

"Guess so," Tye replied and laughed with the rest."

"Anyway, like I said Ben was mad. He searched the ground from his first trap to the last and saw no tracks that he didn't recognize. I did the same where mine were set. We returned to camp a few minutes before the others and had Jim's ear, telling him what happened. Jim agreed it sounded like we had a problem but before going off half cocked; let's wait to see what the others had to say. Bridger, in all the years I knew him, never did anything without thinking things out."

"When the others did come in, they were sure we had someone running our traps. They only had five beaver between them and damn near every trap was sprung. I knew we had a problem for sure now, as did Jim. We skinned and fleshed the plews and had and put them on willow hoops to dry before talking and getting a plan together. We all looked to Jim. This is what we will do, he said. Culhane, you stay here in camp with your guns handy. Jim knew Culhane was not an experienced tracker and would be of more use here in camp. Ben, you and Buff come with me. He knew Stumpy was good at reading sign so he sent him with Grissom and LaCroix. He instructed them to go to their traps, one or two cross the creek and look for sign on the opposite bank while the other man stays on this side looking. That was agreeable with everyone so we left with one more parting word from Jim: if you find tracks don't follow them. Come back and get the rest of us so we can go with you and end this mess. You go off by your lonesome, you may find yourself in more trouble than you can handle. These boys have done this before and know what they are doing. They also know what the penalty is if they get caught, so they will fight."

"When we arrived where our trap line started, Jim and I went across the creek. The water was almost chest deep so we stripped down plum naked and carried our buckskins, guns, and powder horns over our heads. This was spring and the water was ice cold. I was shaking when I reached the other side. We sat in the sun for a few minutes to dry some and then put our buckskins back on. That was the best feeling I had had in a while when those skins, warmed by the sun, touched my cold skin."

"It only took a few minutes to find what we expected to find...tracks going into and out of the water. That's why we could find no tracks on the side we had the traps on...the thieves stayed in the water. We would follow the tracks when the others arrived. Ben left to get them. Jim and me could find no reason to cross back over the creek and then have to come back over here again to follow the men. I know I didn't want to get in that damn icy water any more than I had to. It was almost an hour before Ben returned with the others. LaCroix and Absher were on the same side we were on. I guess they felt the same as we did about the water."

"Ben and Grissom stripped, waded across and come out shivering. After they dressed we followed the tracks, staying in single file so as not to mess up any tracks if Jim, who was in front, lost them and we had to backtrack to find where they left the trail. These men were trappers like us, and knew how to make a trail hard to follow. Following the faint trail was pretty slow going but Bridger was like a fly on horse dung, he wasn't going to get off it."

"It was about an hour later, almost noon, when LaCroix, who was behind Bridger, spotted the smoke coming from a thick cluster of pines. We immediately dropped to a knee to study the situation. We all were quick to note that this wasn't going to be easy. They had a good defensive spot with a little open ground all around them, at least on the sides we could see. We figured the far side of the trees was open too. Like I said, these were no pilgrims we were chasing."

Buff stopped and patted the bowl of his pipe, which had gone out, so the tobacco came out in the palm of his hand. He walked over to the window and tossed the burned tobacco outside, came back and sat down. Jim said, "We may have to wait until dark and try to sneak in on them. Till then, we need to stay out of sight." He told Grissom to go back to camp and tell Culhane what's going on and we may not be in tonight. He told Grissom to stay with him, and make sure no one gets into camp. We will see you late tonight or early in the morning. As soon as Grissom left, we scattered out along the trail on both sides maybe thirty or so yards off it and sat down, out of sight. We all hoped that the thieves had not spotted us through the trees before we dropped to a knee a few minutes ago. We had hardly sat down when we heard three or four shots from the far side of the camp. The breeze was in our faces and the shots fired were faint. We figured them to be at least a half mile or more. We all figured the same thing…there may be another creek over there and the thieves and some honest trappers were having at it or some trappers were in trouble with some Blackfoot. We didn't figure it was the latter of the two but we were going to find out. If it was the Blackfoot, we were not going to let them get to some of our friends if we could help it and we sure as hell wanted to help if it was the thieves. Just as we started running in the direction of the shots, two more rang out."

"We stopped long enough to get a better direction then headed there as fast as we could. There were no more shots and that bothered me and I know it did everyone else. We topped a low hill and saw two men lying on the bank of a creek below us, and three men on horseback riding away leading two packhorses. We hustled down to the men and were shocked to find it was Perkins and Gentry, two of Culhane's friends that had helped us out in the fight with the Blackfoot. Gentry was still alive but not for long. Perkins had been shot twice in the chest and was dead. We poured some water on Gentry's face and his eyes flew open. He recognized me and Jim who were bent over him. He asked about Perkins. We just shook our heads. He looked down at the hole in his belly and knew he was a dead man also. Jim asked him what happened. He struggled for words that were growing fainter with every breath. What he said was Voyageur's came by two days ago trying to recruit them to work with them for some fur company. We told them we were free trappers and liked it that way. Three of them came back this morning and we caught them robbing our traps. He raised his head with great effort and looked at his camp... and cursed. He lay back down and with his last breath said they took all the plews Perkins and he had trapped. He took a deep breath, exhaled slowly, and died."

"Bridger told Ben to stay here at the camp. Told him we were going back to our camp and Buff, Culhane, and himself would be back in the morning with horses and supplies. He said we were going to track those sonofabitches down and kill them before they kill some more of our friends. LaCroix wanted to know why he wasn't coming back. Jim put his hand on the man's shoulder and told him we needed more than one man to watch our camp and besides, these men here were Culhane's friends. He deserves to go. LaCroix nodded and we left, leaving Ben in the camp. The next day we would start something none of us liked…hunting white men, but it had to be done."

Chapter Twenty Four

"Culhane, Bridger, and I mounted our horses at first light and crossed the stream by our camp. We were in the dead men's camp where Ben was less than an hour later. We had Ben's horse with us and enough food and supplies for a week. Ben found a shovel in the trappers camp and buried the two men and placed a crude cross with their names on each. Culhane spent a few minutes by the graves and then come over to us with a look of rage on his face and in his voice. He mounted his horse and said, "Let's go get them bastards, in a voice quivering with anger."

"We crossed the creek and began following the tracks in single file with Jim in front. If a man knows someone is after him, he usually sets a pretty good pace to get away or at least, make an effort to cover his tracks. These men had no idea we were hot on their trail and were taking their time. We found where they stopped for the night only five miles from where they killed the trappers. Reading sign, Jim said they had not been in a hurry to break camp and we were no more than two, maybe three hours behind them. We picked up the pace a little hoping to get this over with quick and get back to our trapping."

"By late afternoon we made a discovery that made us nervous as hell. Three more men jointed the three we were chasing and they had a pack mule. The tracks of the mule were deep indicating a heavy load. We all knew this load was beaver plews from other trappers. By dusk, we were close enough to be careful of not to make any excess noise. We stopped and made camp just a few minutes before full dark. We had one man watching the whole night and no fire. We knew this mess would come to a head shortly after daylight. We, at least I was, were just a might nervous and didn't get a whole lot of sleep that night."

"We were saddled and mounted by the time it was light enough to see. We had gone maybe a mile when Jim, held up his hand signaling us to stop. When he dismounted, we did the same. A second later, we knew why he had stopped...smoke...we smelled the smoke of a campfire. Ben motioned toward some large boulders and we walked our horses to them and picketed them. We took a canteen each and followed Jim on foot toward the camp. Depending on circumstances the fight could be a short one or a siege which could last several hours. That was the reason for each of us carrying a canteen."

"We found the camp on a knoll and bare of any cover we could use to approach it for at least fifty yards in every direction. Like I said before, these were no pilgrims. We discussed several plans of attack but none seemed feasible without getting some of us killed. We were still discussing the situation when Culhane said the men were breaking camp. We looked in the direction of the camp and they were in the process of mounting their horses. Ben said to follow him and when I stop, all of you dismount, kneel and fire. After firing, leave your long rifles on the ground and use your pistols. Ben was one who if he had been in the army, would have been a general. He could come up with a plan quicker than anyone in a pinch...and this was one of those pinches. They were mounting their horses and were a half mile from us."

"Without waiting for any discussion, Ben took off. We were close on his horse's heels. We closed to maybe a hundred yards before they saw us. In a few seconds we were close enough to see their faces showing real fear. When Ben stopped, we stopped, dismounted, kneeled and immediately four fifty caliber balls were on their way toward the thieves. Two men were knocked from their saddles and a horse went down throwing its rider hard onto the rocky ground. Ben was up and running again then stopped with us behind him. We all fired our pistols at the three men riding away. They were fifty yards away and moving away from us fast, not an easy shot for a long rifle and we had pistols. One of us got lucky though as one of the men slumped over his horse's neck. He held on for a few bounds then fell off, hitting the ground like a rag doll. The other two were riding hard, laying low over their saddles."

"Ben grabbed one of the downed thief's long guns and pistol, mounted one of their horses and headed out, hell bent for leather after the two men. The other horses had run off and one was down so we were helpless to go with him. All we could do was wait. We didn't like it with Ben going after two men by himself but there was nothing we could do but go get our horses and follow him and that was going to take a few minutes. The two men shot were dead, but the one whose horse was shot was busted up some, but still alive. Ben was a man who reacted immediately in every situation I ever saw him in and like now, didn't wait to get anyone's approval. He just had a knack for knowing what to do without thinking about it. Not too many men had that."

"The only thing I know what happened during the chase is what Ben told us. He said he was within two hundred yards of the men quickly. The horse he was on loved to run and Ben, figuring it might be a run of a few miles, had to hold him back. Within a few minutes he had closed to a hundred yards. The two men, apparently seeing a lone rider was chasing them, pulled up and took cover behind some boulders. They didn't know just who it was chasing them or they would have kept on going," Buff said laughing.

"Yep! Those boys made a big mistake by stopping, but then knowing Ben the way I did, he would have caught them anyway even if he had to run them down on foot. When he set his mind on doing something there was no stopping him. Anyway, those two bailed off their horses and took up behind some boulders and was going to blast this man plum out of his saddle. The only problem was when they looked, the man had disappeared."

"They were in a fix now. Anytime you don't know where your enemy is and he knows exactly where you are...you have a problem. Ben laughed when he told the story to us later of the two men frantically looking in every direction trying to find him. He was about forty yards away, watching them from behind some thick brush. He had one of them in his sights and hollered for them to throw their guns away. They froze at the sound of his voice but only for a couple of seconds. They jumped to their feet and raised their rifles. Ben fired and saw the ball hit the shortest man square in the chest and knocked him into the bigger man and his shot went harmlessly into the air."

"The man grabbed his pistol and fired it at Ben, but fired too quick and missed. Ben stepped out holding his handgun on the man. Ben said the man dropped his hands to his side as if it was over, but then got the surprise of his life. The man started taunting him, calling him all sorts of vile things. When Ben got close he said the man pulled a knife and challenged him to fight him man to man."

Buff laughed. "This was like waving a red flag in front of a bull. Ben said he thought it over and decided he had rather take this man back alive. He was confident he could handle the man. He knew the man could not be as good as a Blackfoot warrior. Ben stuck the pistol in his belt and pulled his Green River Knife, dropped into a crouch and quickly looked around on the ground to see if there was anything on the ground he might stumble on. Seeing none he motioned for the man to come on. The man came all right...he came like a charging bear and wildly swinging his knife. Ben sidestepped the man and cut him across the buttocks as he went by. The man howled in pain and grabbed his butt with his left hand and when he brought his hand back and looked at it, it was a bloody mess."

"Ben was smiling when he told the rest of the story. The man charged again and this time Ben parried his thrust with his blade and caught the man with a crushing blow square on the chin with a left fist that lifted the man off his feet and deposited him hard on his butt on the ground. The man howled again when his sliced up butt hit the ground. I tell you the truth, when Ben was telling this we were all howling with laughter. The man stood up, threw his knife sticking into the ground in disgust and raised his hands above his head."

"Seeing the man was unarmed Ben stepped forward and reached for the man's arm to turn him around so he could tie him up. Only Ben's reflexes saved him from what happened next. Just as Ben reached for the man's hands, the man came up with a knife from a sheath behind his neck and took a vicious swipe at Ben's throat. Ben stepped back and when the knife passed by and the momentum of the vicious swing had the man slightly off balance, Ben waded in and hit him with rights, lefts, and knees. He beat him to a pulp...damn near beat him to death. He threw the dead man on a horse, tied the half conscious man on his horse, grabbed the reins of the pack horse and headed back to where the camp was. We had rounded up our horses and were following his tracks when we met him coming back. We returned to where the thieves' camp was located. The man who had been thrown from his horse was still there, tied to a tree. We counted over two hundred pelts those men had taken. We took what we figured was ours and kept the rest separate to see what we would do with them at the rendezvous. The trappers would hold court to see what to do with them. Chances are they would tell us to take them. We wanted it to be that way and never be accused of taking someone's plews." Buff leaned back in his chair and looked at Arnold who obviously had a question. "You want to say something, Sergeant Arnold.?"

"Yes sir. I was wondering what you did with the two thieves that wasn't killed?"

"Hell son, we hung them from a damn tree for all to see. Put a sign on them too, telling who ever come across them that this is what happens to thieves. After hanging them we went to our camp and back to what we do best…trapping beavers."

"Over the next seven or so years everything was much the same as the last two years. Over the years trappers came and went in our little group. LaCroix was hurt pretty bad in a scrape with the Utes and decided he had enough of this life and went back to Canada. We had a few scrapes with the Blackfoot and one with a large band of Ute's but they pretty much left us alone. Bridger and I both thought it was because of Ben and his reputation. The five of us, Culhane, Absher, Ben, Jim, and me stayed together.

"There was one fight in '32 that Ben saved Bridger's life and ended our friend, Culhane's. Our camp was attacked one morning at the break of dawn by several Blackfoot warriors. We were already up, moving about camp and that is the only thing that saved our lives…that and Ben." Buff stopped, leaned back and shut his eyes. "I can still see Ben doing what Ben does when he's excited or mad."

"The first of the warriors made the mistake of getting to Ben by himself and met Ben's hatchet that split his head like a melon does when dropped on some rocks. Ben, screaming as loud as the Blackfoot were, picked the dead man up, raised him above his head, threw him ten feet into the charging warriors, knocking three or four down. It caused enough of a distraction that gave us an extra second to get our guns and three more caught the heavy balls of the long rifles. The rest of the 'Red Sticks' were on us. Anytime, as you know Tye, you are in a hand to hand fight with an Indian, it can only be described as hell on earth and we had a whole passel of them on us so you can imagine what it was like."

"There were five of us, Absher, Culhane, Bridger, Ben and myself. I can't rightly say how many Blackfoot there was but there were more than enough to go around. I saw Culhane go down immediately from a blow to the head. I got busy myself with two on me. I killed one with my hatchet and then had a wrestling match with the other trying to keep his knife out of my belly. My hatchet was buried in the head of the one I killed so I only had my knife. We both had good grips on the other's knife hand and was pretty much at a standoff till I did what I had saw Ben do before...butt the man in the face with the top of my head. His grip came loose and I drove my Green River Knife plum to the hilt in his chest."

251

"Absher had killed one but was on his back with a warrior on top of him. I stepped over and pulled the man's head back and slashed his throat. Absher was on his feet instantly and we were immediately attacked by two more of the devils. I took a glancing blow from a club, but managed to drive my knife into the man's belly before everything went black. Absher, who was as quick as any Indian, managed to take care of his attacker with his knife."

"What happened next I can only say what I was told because I was out of the fight. Bridger told me he had killed one with his hatchet and then took an arrow in his hip. He saw Ben swinging and slashing with Indians all over him. He did not know what happened to Ben for a minute because he went down himself with three braves on top of him. Absher stepped over and dispatched one, blowing the top of the man's head off with his pistol, but he was hit with an arrow in his leg and was on the ground. Bridger said he still had two on top of him and thought he was a goner when all of a sudden the two braves were several feet away from him...on their backs. Ben came over and pulled them off, and threw them maybe ten feet saving Jim from a sure death or at least, a nasty wound. The two quickly got to their feet and with the others that were still able, high-tailed it out of our camp with Ben, blood all over his body, chasing them and screaming like some wild animal. Jim said it was a sight he would never forget and he bet those 'Red Sticks' Ben was chasing wouldn't forget it either.

"I was coming around about that time, trying to get my thoughts straight. I saw a hell of lot of bodies strewn all around our camp. Culhane was dead, Absher was down with an arrow through his thigh, Jim had a arrow sticking out of his hip, I had a busted head, and Ben, well, he had cuts from knives on his arms, chest, and belly but none life threatening. I tell you, we were a mess, but we were alive...all but our friend, Culhane. We looked in amazement at the number of dead warriors...fifteen of them, not counting the three we shot before they got into our camp. I think I killed four, Jim two, and Absher two. After recounting the fight with each other, we looked at Ben who was at the creek washing his cuts. We all knew that man had killed at least six or seven Blackfoot warriors in hand to hand fighting and still had the time to pull the two off Bridger. We three had seen a lot in the mountains, but never a man that killed six or seven Blackfoot warriors with a knife and hatchet. I say Ben killed six or seven because in a fight like that everything is a blur and exact number a man killed can vary some, but it's a fact, he killed at least six. Absher made the comment that he was going to have a lot to tell at the next rendezvous about that young man at the creek washing his wounds. I guess the word got around to one of them writers because the next year we heard the story of the fight was in one of those dime novels back east." He chuckled some. "Ben had killed twenty warriors according to the story. That goes back to what I said earlier. Most of the stories in those novels were based on things that actually happened, but liberties were taken with the facts. When the story about the fight was in one of them novels, Ben took a lot of ribbing from the other trappers at the rendezvous over killing twenty Indians with his hands. Ben took it well. He could give a man a hard time with his words, but he could take it also."

"We got the shaft out of Jim's hip but the point came loose and we could not get it out. It stayed in his butt and caused him a lot of misery until the rendezvous of 1836 when a wagon train came through with a real doctor...the first in the mountains that I knew of. He got the tip out after digging down to it with his knife and then he had to use a set of large forceps to break the point away from the hip bone it had become attached to. The tip was steel instead of the usual flint and when entering the hip the point bent around the bone and over the years became attached to the bone. I've told you before that to be a trapper you had to be pretty damn tough. Well, Bridger went through all this until he passed out from the pain without uttering a sound. The only pain killer was some rotgut whiskey that we got down him. That's what I call tough."

"Tye," Buff said. "I don't know what else to tell you about your pa except what other men thought of him. He was such big medicine to the Blackfoot warriors they would go out one at a time to try and kill him. It would make the warrior who did a big man among his fellow warriors. I don't know for sure how many because Ben didn't say much about it but I know for a fact it was at least five because I saw their dead bodies. I would guess it was at least twice that number…maybe more over the years."

"Among the trappers he was one of the most respected men in the mountains. Everyone knew he would help a man anyway he could, but above all else…he was a man of his word. If he told you he would do something, he would do whatever he had to do to do it. I know you know this but he was a man of God and prayed every day. The only man I ever knew that prayed as much as he did was Jedediah Smith."

Buff stood up. "Need to stretch these old legs. I'm going to walk around out side some. Be back in a minute."

When he was outside, Christian commented. "That old man is the most remarkable man I have ever met. To have lived in that country under the conditions he described is beyond my imagination; Indians, snow, below zero weather, thieves, wolf packs, grizzles, and a hundred other things that could kill you…and he loved it!" He shook his head.

255

Arnold laughed and said. "All we have to worry about is Apaches and maybe a rattlesnake biting you on the butt."

Tye laughed with his friends. "Buff was one tough hombre…still is, as both of you have seen. Pa told me a lot of stories over the campfires we shared. Very few of them were about him, mostly about Buff, Absher, and Jim and the things they had done. They were all tough men, and doing what they loved to do. When Rebecca and I were in San Antonio on our honeymoon, we were in a store that had a lot of paintings on the walls. One stuck in my memory. It was a painting of what had to be the Rockies. It was a painting that had to be in the summer and I have never seen such a beautiful place. In the background you could see the mountains that my pa used to describe to me with the snow on the peaks that stayed year around. In the foreground was a small stream, pine trees that looked sixty feet tall and the white barked aspen trees, the ones you have heard Buff say were the prettiest thing God ever created, lining the bank of the creek. Standing in the tall grass of the meadow were several Buffalo. It was a beautiful picture and one that I will never forget."

"Sounds to me like you would like to go there someday," Arnold said.

Tye laughed. "I've thought about it more than once."

"If you go someday, I would like to go with you," Christian said.

"You're in the army," Tye said smiling.

"I'd resign or desert to go to those mountains."

Tye laughed. "I don't think either of us is tough enough to handle it."

"You're like your pa, Tye...plenty tough enough to go."

"He was," Tye answered. "They all were. They were a special breed of man, different from normal folks who wanted a family, a roof over their heads, and a job that would allow them to give their family what they wanted and needed. A normal man knew that tomorrow was a work day and he would leave to go to his job or to the fields, and would be back for an evening meal and be with his family and do it again the next day. Sunday was a day of rest and he and his family would go to Church and visit with friends or relatives. The mountain man probably never actually knew what day of the week or month is was for sure. He knew winter, spring, summer, and fall...trapping season and resting season. Most could not read or write but they could tell you what the weather was going to be tomorrow. They could look at the stars and tell you what time it was within a half hour or so which to them was close enough. They could leave one camp and travel a hundred miles on unmarked trails, through winding canyons, over mountains, and come back to the exact spot they had left. Their memory of the lay of the land led to maps that would later mark the way for thousands of travelers going west to California. Some of the trails like the one through the South Pass are allowing wagon trains to pass through on their way to the Pacific Northwest right now. I believe it will be proven in a few years just what an impact the mountain man had on the history of this country."

Buff came back in and sat down at the table. "I was telling the boys here what an impact I believe history will show you and men like Bridger and pa had on this country," Tye said.

"I don't know about that, Tye. I hope what we did is remembered. We explored a lot of land that no white man had seen. A lot of that knowledge was used later by men like Bridge, Coulter, and Jed Smith in mapping trails that turned into roads through the Rockies. A hell of a lot pf people in wagons have passed through the mountains going west that could not have found their way without the trails."

"I've told you a lot of stories about your pa, Tye. There were a lot more but the ones I told you about I remember the best. We trapped together for ten years before the demand for beaver fell off and it was just not worth the time and trouble anymore. I had about twenty-five hundred dollars when I quit trapping. That wasn't much for twenty years or so of work but I would not have traded those years for anything a man could offer me. I saw a lot of men in my travels after that that had been working for a long time and had nothing to show for it, so I felt blessed. I still have most of it. I just never was one was to spend a lot of money on foolish things. I spent a little on whiskey, women, and cards, but nothing foolish," he said slapping the table with the palm of his hand and laughing with everyone else.

When the laughter was over he looked at Christian and Arnold. Buff spoke in a more somber voice. "I came here to Fort Clark to see my friend's son and to tell him about his pa. I have done that. I can also tell you, Tye, just how proud of you Ben would have been for what you have done and will do. From what I have heard from men here at Clark, and seen with my own eyes you have what us mountain men would say, "The Hair of the Bear." That's the highest praise a mountain man can give a fellow trapper. Ben was that and so are you." The old mountain man's eyes misted over a bit. "He was my friend and I am proud to have known him. I just wish I could have seen him one more time before he went and got his self killed." He stood up and excused himself. He was a little embarrassed at the emotion that had come over him. Tye stood and caught him before he left the room and took the little man in his arms and pulled him to his chest.

In a voice filled with emotion, Tye said, "Pa loved you the same way, Buff. He always said he would never have been what he was without you. There was never a night around a campfire your name did not come up. Your being here now is nothing short of a miracle and you, as Rebecca and me have told you before, will always be here as long as you want to be. You are family."

Epilogue

For several days, Tye thought about the stories Buff had told him about his pa trapping in the Rockies. He had wondered about Absher and Bridger and what happened to them and he had asked Buff about them. Buff told him Absher was still scouting for the Army in Colorado, and the last he heard, Bridger had founded Fort Bridger on the Green River in 1841 and was still there as far as he knew. The fort was a stopping place for travelers' on their westward journey. They could rest and have their wagons refurbished at the blacksmiths in the fort. Jim also scouted for the army part time and in 1850, showed the representatives of the Union Pacific Railroad a way though the mountains which became know as Bridger's Pass, or by some as the South Pass. The railroad carried thousands through the Rockies. Last Buff heard was that Bridger was still alive and kicking.

Years proved what Tye thought about history and the effect of the mountain man had on this country. The main result of their adventures was continent exploration which advanced the westward expansion of this great land. Without their knowledge and willingness to share it, the westward expansion would have been delayed by years.

History show that approximately 3,000 trappers were in the mountains from 1820 until 1840. In those twenty years though, no more than a few hundred were in the mountains at any one time. Indians, grizzlies, drowning in rivers, starvation, and the severe winters took their toll. Some didn't make it one year and others left after realizing the life of a trapper was dangerous, arduous, and sometimes just damn miserable and very few were going to get rich.

The fur companies did well though, as an average of 200,000 dollars a year in pelts was sent back east. This was not counting the furs of bear, buffalo, fox, wolves, and a dozen other animals that were sold. The average trapper could count on 200 to 350 pelts a year and after selling them to the traders at the rendezvous and buying the over priced supplies, had little money left. The hard core trappers like Buff and his group had their wealth though in the beautiful Rockies and freedom to do what they wanted and when they wanted to do it.

~

Two weeks later, Bill Baxter, was well enough physically to be escorted by Tye and a small detachment of soldiers from Clark to Fort Inge where the outlaw was to hang with his brother, Robert and his nephew, James. Todd Jenkins rode with them also. He insisted he wanted to see the men who killed his family receive their just reward.

The two day trip was without incident and the day after they arrived, the three men were hung on the gallows. Just as Tye figured, young Todd could not watch the men die. He left the crowd that was gathered and sobbed when he heard the trap doors, dropping the men to their just reward.

Tye came over and put his arm around the boy. He told Todd it was over, and he had to get on with his life. He told him not to feel ashamed he didn't want to watch men die. He explained he was the same way, and seldom watched the men he brought in hang. Getting on with his life is what his parents and sister would want. He told him the O'Malley's wanted him to stay with them, to be part of their family.   Tye told him that he thought this would be a good idea and he would personally teach him things like tracking, reading sign, and other things he would need to know to survive this country. Together, they would make trips to the Jenkins homestead and take care of the graves of his parents and sister. Todd knew that Tye and Dan had gone back to where his sister was temporarily buried and took her body and buried it next to her parents. They would also keep the place livable so when Todd wanted to, he could move there and continue what his parents had started.

Todd thought about the things Tye said on their way back to Fort Clark. He rode his horse up beside Tye's the morning of the second day just before they arrived back at Clark. He said he thought the idea of staying with the O'Malley's was a good one on one condition; Tye would start teaching him immediately all that he would need to know to make it in this land. His life so far had been raising cattle, goats, and other farm critters and he knew all of the ins and outs of that business but nothing of what Tye could teach him and he was excited and could not wait to start. Tye was happy because he would finally have a chance to do what his pa had done for him, pass some of his knowledge and experience to someone else. With Rebecca still a few months away from having their baby and then waiting a few more years for his son, if it was a son, to be old enough to start learning what Tye could teach him, he was ready to start this young man's 'education' immediately…and he would.

Gary McMillan

Breinigsville, PA USA
29 March 2010
235070BV00002B/5/P